SEP 0 5 2007

# STRANGE
# SKIES

# STRANGE SKIES

## A NOVEL

## MATT MARINOVICH

HARPER PERENNIAL

NEW YORK ● LONDON ● TORONTO ● SYDNEY

HARPER ● PERENNIAL

P.S.™ is a trademark of HarperCollins Publishers.

STRANGE SKIES. Copyright © 2007 by Matt Marinovich. All rights reserved. Printed in the United States of America. No part of this book may be used or reproduced in any manner whatsoever without written permission except in the case of brief quotations embodied in critical articles and reviews. For information address Harper-Collins Publishers, 10 East 53rd Street, New York, NY 10022.

HarperCollins books may be purchased for educational, business, or sales promotional use. For information please write: Special Markets Department, HarperCollins Publishers, 10 East 53rd Street, New York, NY 10022.

First Edition

*Designed by Nancy Singer Olaguera, ISPN Publishing Services*

Library of Congress Cataloging-in-Publication Data is available upon request.

ISBN: 978-0-06-123391-3
ISBN-10: 0–06–123391-9

07  08  09  10  11   ISPN/RRD   10  9  8  7  6  5  4  3  2  1

For Marian

# ACKNOWLEDGMENTS

I'D LIKE TO thank my editor, John Williams, and my agent, Byrd Leavell. A first novel couldn't have better friends.

# STRANGE
# SKIES

# CHAPTER 1

I'VE ALWAYS FOUND it hard to have a normal conversation with my brother's wife when she's breastfeeding. In fact, I find it hard to have a normal conversation with Terry when she's *not* breastfeeding. Add the breast to the picture, and that saliva-encrusted rug slug she calls her baby boy, and I just go blank. My wife, Lee, I notice, can go on talking as if it were perfectly natural. My older brother, with his thinning blond hair and outdated goatee, doesn't really notice anything anymore. Eric's brain is in some kind of septic kid shock. They have three of them already, and to make ends meet, since Terry doesn't work, he's gambling online fourteen hours a day. Through some quirk of the system he clears about three thousand bucks a month, but his expressions have this strange automatic quality that rarely connect with anything that's being said. No matter what I say, I just feel like I'm dealing him another virtual face card.

We're sitting in a living room in South Orange, New Jersey. You can picture it. An old Victorian with vinyl siding, planted next to two other old Victorians with vinyl siding, a bunch of gruesomely colored toys lying on their sides in the patch of front yard, a dozen *New York Times* still wrapped tight in blue plastic on the front stoop because they don't have the time to read, or go to the movies, or even take a shower, and then you open the front door, with its depressing frosted glass design, and the smell hits you. Last night's grease fire, which is what Terry has been going on about.

"And all of a sudden I look up," she says, bouncing once on the couch to get her breast in the baby's mouth again, "and the whole stove is on fire."

"Literally," Eric says. He's sitting on a chair near the dining room table, hunched over, with a Sierra Nevada in his hand.

"What happened?" my wife shouts. I love Lee, but she drives me nuts. Disasters just excite her too much. Any kind of disaster will do. Sometimes, enjoying my first cup of coffee, I'll hear a low murmuring and realize that Lee is reading off the names of the latest soldiers who have been killed in action in Iraq. What am I supposed to do with this information? Bad luck is just bad luck. My brother's grease fire. Don't want to hear about it.

But I'm listening. I'm looking at my watch. Terry is

still talking. The baby is still sucking. My brother still hasn't taken a sip of his beer.

"His whole head could have caught fire," Terry says. And then something strange happens: Eric smiles, just a little, and I know he wouldn't have minded if his whole head caught fire. It would have hurt, yes, no doubt about it. But he would have finally had a decent reason to escape this misery, if only for a moment, as he ran, flaming, across his own lawn. Free for a few yards, at least, before he collapsed.

"Close call," I say, letting my eyes dip down toward the baby, who glares at me greedily with his glittering blue eyes, his damp brown hair swept to one side, Hitler-style.

"Very close call," Terry says. Her face is not unpretty, despite the oily black bangs, but the rest of her body has become oblong. You could push her over and she'd come bouncing right back up again.

"You just have to be on guard every minute," Lee says. "You never know what's going to happen. You just have to be on guard."

Lee, on the other hand, is not oblong. It's October, but somehow she's retained the last of her summer tan, her curly blond hair pulled back tight, blinking her green eyes at the baby, teasing its fat hand with the handle of a rattle, which it immediately sticks into its mouth.

3

It doesn't have to be like this. Just a few months ago, we were doing fine. We'd decided to hike New Zealand. On the top of a glacier, we'd stared into each other's mirrored sunglasses, multiplying our sense of adventure. And then she planted a ski pole into the crusty ice and ruined everything. She told me she wanted to start a family. I hiked back in angry silence, doing my best to find a hidden crevasse.

I'm staring at her now, trying to catch her eye, knowing that she's about to cave in and tell Eric and Terry about the thing they removed from my bicep. Some stupid lump. An adnexal carcinoma. And yes, I'm going in tomorrow to get the results of the sentinel node excision and yes, there's a small chance it might have spread to my lymphatic system, but this isn't the time or the place. I'm perfectly healthy, and I'd like, if possible, to wind things up in New Jersey, not get lost in Newark like last time, and get back to Park Slope before it starts to rain. Clouds have been thickening all day, and as I look through the windows, I notice it's getting darker. The color gray, sitting on everything.

"Paul," Lee says, giving me a knowing look. "Do you want to tell them?"

"You're pregnant!" Terry shouts, bouncing on the couch again, the airlock broken between her child's mouth and her nipple. A jet of human milk arcs through the air and lands on the pink carpet.

"Congratulations," my brother says, half-raising that bottle of beer.

Besides trying to catch his head on fire, Eric has taken up smoking again. Cigarettes *and* pot. As we stand on the sagging back porch, he takes a joint out of the Marlboro Lights box, flips it onto his lips, and lights up.

"Here," he says, handing it to me.

"I can't," I say. "I'm driving."

"So what?" he says. "It's not like you have three kids strapped to the backseat."

I take a small hit and hand it back to him.

"Must be nice to have a grill," I say, nudging my chin toward the rusted hulk of steel parked near the dying peach tree. That's about the only perk I can see as far as this whole parent thing goes. Your grill and your giant TV.

"Causes cancer," Eric says. "That's what the experts say. The way it cooks the meat or something. So Terry won't let me use it anymore. We're into this silk tofu stuff. You ever had silk tofu?"

"Fuck off."

"I'm serious. Don't be such a hard-ass. Pretty soon you're going to be walking in my shoes, baby brother."

"I could just walk away," I say dreamily. "I could just kiss Lee on the cheek one morning and get in the Mazda."

Few people have ever substituted the word *Mazda* for the word *freedom*. I am one of those people. No matter how trapped I feel, I always have that car. And it can still take me anywhere.

Eric tosses the joint on the porch. I wait for him to crush it out with his sneaker, but he doesn't, he just lets it burn. Taking the Zippo out of his pocket he lights a cigarette for himself and hands me one.

"You're full of shit," Eric says. "Lee's great. Besides, her mother's loaded. You're going to cut out before you inherit the mother load?"

"She wants kids," I say, feeling the pained expression begin around my eyebrows. "She wants like three or four of them. I can't do it. I *hate* kids."

"That," Eric says behind a wreath of smoke, "is intensely sad."

"Eric," I say, waving my arm at the decrepitude around us, "*this* is intensely sad. You can't even flip a hamburger on your own grill."

"One day," he says, dragging deeply on the cigarette while simultaneously kicking the burning roach into an unraked pile of dead leaves, "you're going to understand. There's love here. And that's all that matters."

Long ago I learned that a man can say one thing and do another. My father, for instance, was a family man to a fault, but managed to sleep with 573 women while he was married. My mother found their names and other vital information in a brown leatherbound book after he died. So that's why I pretend to listen to my brother, but keep a firm eye on the desiccated leaves, waiting to see if the whole pile ignites.

"Yeah," my brother says, nodding sanctimoniously, then wincing at the first drop of rain. "You don't know anything about love."

For a few minutes, Lee and I sit in the old Mazda, letting the motor run. I briefly glance at my face in the rearview mirror and realize that I look as outdated as my brother. A lolling tongue of brown hair splits my forehead, and it looks like I haven't slept for days, which is true.

I've been thinking about the next step. I've been thinking about kids. A family. The future. And I can't come up with a single good excuse not to have them that wouldn't sound ridiculous to Lee.

I look gray, and it's not just because of the rain. I've seen the future, and it's screaming inside that Victorian, farting inside its I'M THE BOSS jumpsuit, eating its adorable little hand.

You wake up one morning, eighteen years later, and realize your life is over. You take your ragged-looking wife on a short cruise, gamble the last of your savings away, get a black belt in silence, and drive fourteen hours to Utica to visit your spawn on Thanksgiving, pass on the coffee, and plow into an oak tree on the way home.

Tell me I'm wrong.

I bend the mirror away from my face, so that I'm looking out the rear window at a pile of wet leaves on my brother's street, the blue and gray recycling bins, a tilted utility pole.

Terry and Eric have already waved good-bye and closed the frosted glass door. The rain has already started to beat down on the roof of the car, squiggles of it moving across the windshield. Rain shadows even drip down Lee's face, accentuating her real sadness.

"I couldn't even tell them the truth," she says.

"About what?" I say. "The cancer or the fact that you're not pregnant?"

"Both."

"I don't want to talk about the cancer. I get the results tomorrow. I don't want to make a big deal of it."

"I'm sorry," she says.

"I mean," I say, "what can I do? All I can do is wait."

Lee's holding my hand now. Rain shadows dribble down our fingers.

"I know you're going to be okay," she says.

"Thanks."

"And once you're okay, I want to get pregnant. I want to have a baby."

There's no point in arguing with her. There's no

point in re-creating what we just saw. When my wife has made an important decision she always hold hands with me for some reason, and then she squeezes, just to let me know how serious she is. There's really only one thing I can possibly say.

"I guess we'll just have to wait for tomorrow."

# CHAPTER 2

THE WAITING ROOM on the third floor of the Mount Zion Cancer Institute is packed. I've been flipping through an issue of *ESPN Magazine,* some backdated interview with Demetrius Davenport, the famous wide receiver. But understandably, I lose focus after the first few questions—I mean, I have *cancer.* And I'm waiting to find out if it's *spread.* And if so, I'm probably going to die. And everyone else in the waiting room has cancer. This very attractive woman sitting in the leather chair on my right, who looks a little like Amy Grant, with the Theory shopping bag planted beside her. That pale man near the plate-glass window in the wheelchair, with his whole family arranged around him, writing down a list of questions they're going to ask the doctor. The middle-aged Asian woman just staring straight forward, forefinger and thumb framing her face in the shape of an *L.*

I turn to another page of the Davenport interview, something about his work with the Wish-on-a-Star Foundation, something about his coach, something about his coming a long way since the bullies in the playground used to beat him up and call him Pig-eye, the origin of which is too painful for him to discuss. Then there's a two-page spread of Demetrius, half-naked, looking completely sculpted and indestructible, and I try to imagine him getting cancer, try to imagine the pages of a fictitious magazine called *Dying Athlete*, but in my mind, I still can't make Demetrius look like he's going to die. Even hooked up to an oxygen tank, even surrounded by family as he lies in his hospital bed, he looks like he's just faking a fatal illness. I know he's probably just banged some groupie in the wheelchair-accessible bathroom and his whole posse has taken over the family waiting room, legs kicked up on chairs, cell phones squawking. Demetrius is simply waiting for me to stop imagining him. He doesn't have the time.

"Excuse me," the woman sitting next to me says. "Do you have the time?"

I do have the time. But it's not on my wrist. It's buried deep in the leather satchel that Lee bought me for my thirty-eighth birthday. I'm smiling back at her as I rummage through each pocket for my cell phone. Two people with cancer, sitting in a waiting room, the least I can do is come up with the time. Besides, she's kind of a knockout, with that curly brown hair, tight little body, perfectly flared jeans, and nifty black boots. Not Upper East Side exactly. I'm guessing Murray Hill, after about five years on the Lower East Side. And her boyfriend, whoever he is, is probably making real cash, unlike me. But this is the key thing: he's not here.

"Found it," I say, still smiling up at her. I've got it in my hand, I'm opening it to get the time, and she's still giving me that sweet, patient look.

"Alex Hivinshki," the nurse says, and she stands up, grabbing her Theory bag, and I'm left staring at the leather chair.

"Good luck," she says to me before turning away, walking soundlessly across the purple and light green carpet toward the doctors' offices, a short, pleasant-looking nurse opening the door for her and lightly touching her elbow.

I'm staring at the time on my cell phone—10:37—and I realize something important.

I don't want to be okay.

I don't want to get Lee pregnant. I don't want to be my brother, trying to catch his head on fire. I want to be with Alex Hivinshki. And if not her, that redhead by the potted plant will do. Or even that stern Asian woman whose face is still welded to her fingers.

Or maybe not, I think, as she wearily closes her eyes, sucks in a lungful of air, and sighs.

• • •

I'm sitting in the small examining room, shirtless, staring at myself in the full- length mirror bolted to the wall. Nothing unusual about that. I've stared at myself in full-length mirrors in lots of examining rooms, stepped on the scale, rifled through the drawers, pumped up a blood pressure cuff, but this morning I'm a little distracted. This examining room is just one in a whole corridor of examining rooms, and through the paper-thin Sheetrock I can hear Dr. Tolson slowly making his way toward me, opening a door, introducing himself to a patient, and then closing the door again. He even uses the same catchphrase: *How are we doing today?* And I don't hear the response to this until he opens the door of the examining room next to mine, and I realize that Alex Hivinshki has been sitting a few feet away from me the whole time. I can make out the tone of her voice immediately. I can hear Dr. Tolson tell her he got the results of the mammogram back and he's a little concerned. I hear her ask him how serious it is and then he goes into a long explanation about differentiated cancer cells I can't understand. I'm not paying attention to that anyway because Alex is weeping. Not loud, out of control sobbing, more like a flash flood he helps to dry up as soon as it starts.

"Thanks," Alex says.

He must have handed her a Kleenex.

"Alex," he says, letting a long pause underline her name. "You're going to be fine. We're going to take care of you."

He gives her a few more instructions, asks her if she has any questions, and then he's gone. There's a warning knock on the door of my examining room. The door opens, and I look him right in the eye, adjusting my gaze a foot downward because he's a short guy, already pumping my hand. I'm not going to pieces, that's for sure. Let me have it. Let the first day of the rest of my dying life begin! At least I can avoid having a kid. You get cancer, you automatically get selfish prick status, and the beautiful thing is that they call it courage.

"Paul," he says, throwing a folder on the small desk and opening it, giving some extremely sloppy handwriting a brief glance. "You passed the test."

"No spread?" I say.

"The sentinel node came back negative," he says, his broad face breaking into a proprietary grin. "You're A-OK."

"Are you sure?" I say.

"Go on," he says, as if he were making my day. "Get out of here. Just schedule a chest X-ray and a follow-up appointment. I'll see you in six months."

"But there's a five percent chance the test missed something. You said that at the beginning."

"Paul," Dr. Tolson says, slightly irritated. "The test came back negative for spread. Do you *want* cancer?"

Just like that, I'm back to normal. Lee will be delighted. In a week, we'll start trying. In a year, we'll probably be spending Christmas with my brother, flashing our cameras at our babies' drooling chins, folding dirty diapers like origami, trading stories of other nearly averted disasters. I'll be standing on that porch with my brother, kicking roaches and burning cigarettes into that same pile of inflammable leaves.

But you could just leave her, I tell myself, drifting into the elevator. No, I can't leave Lee. I love Lee, I really do. And the money. I have to be smart about that. Who in his right mind walks away from the possibility of inheriting two million dollars? There has to be another way out.

"You okay?" Alex says from the back of the elevator.

"Me," I say, stabbing the LL button. "I'm fine."

"You're shellshocked, too," she says. "I can tell. You pressed the wrong button."

I press three more buttons before I finally get the right one, and we both laugh each time the elevator opens to an empty floor.

"It sucks," I say. I might as well play along, if it makes her feel better.

I have never, in my entire life, uttered two words that made such an instant impression. At first, I think they have no effect at all, but when the elevator doors finally open on the right floor and I step off and start walking away, trying to think of one more nice thing to say, Alex grabs my hand.

"You're coming with me," she says with a warm smile. I must be blushing like a schoolkid as she leads me through the sliding glass doors and the jumble of wheelchairs assembled there. I don't say a word until she's climbed into the back of a taxi and pulled me in.

"Where we going?" the driver says.

"Twenty-third and Lex," Alex says, staring at me.

The driver pulls into traffic and immediately hits a red light. Alex is kissing my ear. My chin. My eyebrow. It's lunch hour and people in business suits are glaring through the windshield, some smiling, some shaking their heads.

"I've never done this before," she says, frisking my crotch with her long, strong fingers.

"I haven't either," I say, as her whole hand disappears inside my fly, the driver glancing in his rearview mirror.

"There's got to be some upside to dying."

"Alex," I should say, because I'm not some opportunistic cad, at least up to now. "I'm not dying."

But I don't say anything. If this is grief, I want

more of it. All these years, I'd gotten nowhere being the picture of health.

"Easy back there," the driver says. "This isn't *Taxicab Confessions*. There aren't any hidden cameras in here."

Alex hands him her whole purse and tells him to take what he wants and shut up.

"Keep on kissing me," she says, diving back in. "If we stop I'm going to cry."

I had never cheated on Lee. I'd thought about it. I'd talked to a few women at some bars until they asked me about the ring on my finger. I'm not the kind of guy who would take the ring off, tell you he wasn't married, look into your eyes, and lie to your face.

But as I walk through the lobby of 434 East Twenty-third Street, my lips crusty from Alex's kisses, my privates still aching from seven kinds of attention (I didn't know there were more than two or three), I feel like I've just lost my virginity again. Some of you must know that feeling. Suddenly the world and all its clever schemes to entrap you seem silly and harebrained. There's that strange sense of power. It's not like you've been elected to office or anything. But you have behind-the-scenes knowledge, and everyone you pass in the street smiles or shies away from you, because they know you're temporarily indestructible.

Why on earth has it taken me so long to realize what I need to do? And who I am? Thirty-eight years old and only now it occurs to me that I'm a born liar.

I take the cell phone out of my pocket and call Lee.

"I've been trying to reach you," she says. She's angry, but it's just a thin layer of anger. Under that centimeter of ice is worried love. "I left fifteen messages."

"I had to take a walk," I say. "I had to think."

"What do you mean?" she says.

I don't say anything for about thirty seconds. And this is the most difficult part, because Lee starts to sob on the other end. I have to restrain myself. I want to tell her I'm fine. I want to tell her I'm A-OK. A part of me does.

The other part just listens to her weep. The other part of me tells her we'll get through this. I tell her that it has spread to my lymph nodes. I tell her Dr. Tolson is giving me a fifty percent chance of survival. But obviously, kids are out. Having a family is out. This will change everything.

"I understand," she says, her voice laboring under all those tears and snot. "I love you."

"I'll be right home," I say.

"Come *right* home," she says. "Don't do something silly."

I say goodbye and take a moment to gather myself. Make sure my fly is zipped, and then I join the rest of you, the crush of you at rush hour, shoulder to shoulder on this warm October sidewalk, behaving the way you think you should.

Most people, I think, go through their whole lives vaguely pretending they're nicer than they really are. My father, for instance, with his 573 women. I look at my recent conversion to bad guy another way. At least I know who I am. After thirty-eight years, it's all making sense, all the loose ends that had driven me crazy before.

Why, for instance, had I helped Derek Dafoe lash Arthur Milgram to a light pole in Central Park when I was in elementary school? With his own tie!

Why had I applied marmalade to my penis one lazy summer afternoon and begged Fonzie, our nervous little cocker spaniel, to lick it off? Which she did, reappearing later that evening at the dinner table, where everyone noticed her matted, sugary fur.

Why, a year ago, when I found a wallet lying on the sidewalk, had I quickly removed the cash before tossing it into a mailbox?

Why had I left the scene after crashing into that parked car in Park Slope, a wrecked headlight still pinned to the Mazda's bumper?

Now, in just under an hour, I had solved everything.

I'm out for myself. And so are you. The only difference is that one of us has stopped lying about that fact.

I've left the old Paul behind. The guy who always told Lee the truth. The guy who was going to get her pregnant. The guy who always told himself her mother's money didn't matter, when it did. The guy who was going to wind up as miserable as Eric, getting self-righteous on a sagging back porch, blinking at the first drops of rain, telling anyone who'll listen that *there's love here.*

*Keep it.* Being nice was so exhausting. If having serious cancer is this much fun, I'm not ever going to be healthy again.

## CHAPTER 3

I WORK AT the Monarch Health Insurance Company in
Englewood Cliffs, New Jersey. For an hour and a half
each day, which is the length of my commute from
and to Brooklyn, I have plenty of time to read a book,
plan the rest of my life, or just try to catch some sleep.
But today, on the PATH train, all I can do is sit and
smile. In fact, I'm still in a great mood by the time I
get to work. For the last six months I've been training
a girl named Lisa Hunt to handle customer accounts.
Everyone at the company knows that the normal training period is three months. Everyone wonders why I
haven't complained. For six months, I've endured the
slightly damp, overweight Lisa Hunt, and her wheez-
ing, and her mountain of pills that she has to transfer
from her desk to mine every morning because she has
diabetes. And then the wheezed apologies. Because
Lisa Hunt, I'm convinced, has a crush on me. She

knows that when her training period ends, her time with me will end as well, so she forgets everything as soon as I say it. All right, maybe not as soon as I say it, but by the next day. So we start over, again and again, and up to now I've endured it because I had this faint notion that I was some kind of nice guy, and that a nice guy would endure this, perhaps forever.

A nice guy.

The idea of that makes my smile really take off as I walk by the receptionist. For six months, I've nodded my head, ignored Lisa's coffee breath, and let her wipe my computer screen and tell me how patient I was. And once, I even let her put her hand on my knee. It's the size of a Little League catcher's mitt, dimples where the knuckles should be. I was so nice that even Lisa Hunt thought she could have me.

This morning, I lean back in my swivel chair, boot up my computer, and wait for Lisa to appear, staring at my desk, which I ritually clean to make sure that I'm not leaving behind any incriminating evidence of myself. I notice, however, that on a small Post-it, left over from Friday, I've written the following fact: "The weight of all the ants in the world is equal to the weight of the entire human race."

I reach out and crumple the note, tossing it in the garbage. I can hear the sound of Lisa's pill bottles, rattling like castanets, before I see her. She appears in my cubicle with her medications balanced on the ledge of her arm. She puts them down one by one and then goes back for her own chair.

This morning I don't say a word. I click on the spreadsheets until I find the one we were working on on Friday.

"Hold on, Speedy Gonzales," Lisa says, unscrewing her pill bottles one by one, readying her cup of water. Then pill. Sip. Gulp. Pill. Sip. Gulp.

"So here we are," I say, nudging my chin at the spreadsheet on my computer screen. "Your customer has called in and asked you about POS for DFOG. What do you enter?"

Her hand is on my leg.

"Something's different about you," she says. "You get a haircut?"

"What do you enter?"

"So serious," she purrs. "Okay, let me concentrate. DFOG. I already forgot what that stands for."

Lisa's kneecap rolls up on my leg like a small boulder. Even if I wanted to push it away, I wouldn't be able to get my fingers around it. She reaches into her tote bag, pulls out her glasses, puts them on, and draws closer to my computer.

"Which line are we on?"

This is the glory of having serious cancer. I just don't have time for this anymore. I click the spreadsheets closed one by one, until we are left with the screen-saver, some hokey painting of a farmhouse in winter, the lights on, the sun just setting, a child in a red jacket and wool cap walking back home. Back when I was a nice guy, this kind of shit made me feel safe. *What was I thinking?*

"We're done," I say.

"But we're not even started," she says. "I haven't even gotten us our coffee."

She means the awful coffee machine stuff. One day, Lisa had pressed all the buttons in a fit of frustration and discovered that the machine would create a double espresso hot chocolate. Not wanting to offend her, I had let her bring me a cup. Every morning.

"You mean that espresso hot chocolate shit?" I say.

You've got to try this some time. I mean those of you who try too hard to be nice anyway, but realize that you've always had some loose ends, some *questions* about who you really are.

Lisa is too shocked to say a word. I, on the other hand, am just getting started.

"Sure, get me a cup," I say. "Press all those crazy buttons. *Tcccchhh.*"

I'm pressing imaginary buttons on an imaginary coffee machine. I'm imitating steam.

"Lisa," I say, "do you really think I'm going to fuck you?"

There are certain phrases that can literally bring my fellow employees' conversations to a halt. In that respect, an office is a very strange place. There are seemingly important conversations, even heated ones, taking place all the time, but the minute you get a little bit personal, all systems shut down. Everyone, for the first time, seems to be listening to you.

A weird humming silence. Tommy Truro has even turned off the tiny Chinese waterfall that sits near his laser printer.

"I'm sorry," I say, as Lisa's face—the corner of her mouth, then her nose, then her forehead—begins to spasm. With a big woman, you can really see it coming. I stand up before she falls apart, and then I walk into my boss's office.

"No *wonder* you flipped on Lisa," Greg Boyden says. "*Dude.*"

"The big C," I say, letting my shoulders sag.

Greg is one of those eternal frat boy types: short hair, strong handshake, and *dude*. All day, that word leaks out of his office. Dude. Dude. Dude. And that word is a fossil. It's a paw print stuck on some rock. Who says that anymore?

But this is a health insurance company. We're all stuck in time. Different times. Tommy Truro actually has the nerve to play Nirvana, softly, on Fridays.

"Jesus, dude. Are you going to be all right?"

"I don't know. It metasta. It meta-sta-tas-sta-tized."

"What?"

If I'm going to have serious cancer, I'm going to have to nail that word on the first try. It's a word that someone with cancer would definitely know how to pronounce.

"When it spreads," I say. "To other parts of your body. Like your bones. Whatever."

"It's in your bones?"

"It's in a bunch of places," I say. Why not?

"Dude," Greg says. "I am so sorry. I'll tell Tim. You're going to need some time off."

"I feel like I'm bailing on you guys. The whole training thing."

"We'll dump her on Tommy, dude," he says. "No problem. Your health comes first."

"Anyway," I say. "I guess I owe Lisa an apology."

"I'll handle it," Greg says, standing up and then gently clapping me on the shoulder. "Just go home."

For a second, I feel guilty. It's too easy. But then I get it. Greg's made my day. But I've made his, too. Serious cancer, especially when you don't have it, is win-win. Greg feels terrific because he's gotten a little bonus lift—he's not a goner, like me! It's like a pyramid scheme that actually works. Five minutes in Greg's office and I'm already on an extended vacation. Back at my cubicle, I collect a few last things from my metal desk drawers and stare at that mawkish screensaver one more time.

Run home, you little wimp, I'm thinking. I'm headed in the other direction.

Those of you who are still with me—those of you who might be thinking, *Hey, maybe it's time I got cancer*—let me give you a word of warning. It's very illuminating. It'll tell you more than you would ever want to know about the friends you have.

My brother called me up drunk. He told me how much he loved me. I could hear one of his kids having a meltdown in the background.

"I'm not dead yet," I said through the noise.

"One second," he said sadly. "Ben just head-butted his sister."

My brother shouted something at his kids and then, in a sorrowful voice, asked me what I just said.

"I said I'm not dead yet."

"Hold on."

There was another commotion, and then my brother yelling at Terry.

"Can you fucking take care of that? My fucking brother has cancer."

"You're drunk," she yelled back at him. "And you're using that as an excuse."

"I'm going to kill her," my brother said softly. "I'm going to come with you."

"What are you talking about?"

"To the other side," my brother said, with eerie conviction. "I'm ready."

After I finished talking with my brother, I called everyone else I knew, just to make it official.

Jack Duarte, my old full-of-shit college roommate, gave me a pep talk.

"You are going to beat this," he said, spluttering with conviction. "Do you hear me?"

"I hear you, Jack," I said, enjoying another sip of the single-malt Scotch that my father-in-law had sent me. The tasteful gifts and polite cards were just starting to pour in.

"Don't be a wimp about this. This is going to require balls. This is going to require, like, elephant sack."

He was one of several friends who just seemed to like to hear themselves talk. Human beings are a frail, vulnerable bunch. Giving comfort to someone with a serious illness is one of the few things we can do that actually makes us feel powerful. Godlike, even. Because the person with the serious illness is even more frail and vulnerable. They're saying, Please, ridiculous human, act like a god. Tell me I'm going to be okay.

So you get elephant sack.

So you get happy survival stories of other relatives with cancer.

So you get the other relatives with cancer. Calling you at dinnertime.

"Hey Uncle Ted," I say.

"Is this a bad time?" he says.

I can't lie. Since getting serious cancer, there haven't been any bad times. Lee's made my favorite, spinach soufflé. It's imploding gently on the table right now, and she's waving for me to hurry.

"No, it's good to hear from you," I say.

Ted has cancer. Bad cancer. It started in his lung and now it's popped up in his liver. I can hear the short bursts of the oxygen machine behind him.

"Eric called me. He told me to call you. Healthy people, they have this idea we should all be in the same kind of club or something."

"The death club," I say, raising my glass of Scotch in a toast.

"I'll tell you one thing," he says. "I don't know if it will help."

"Shoot," I say, raising my eyebrows at Lee, so she knows I'm winding the conversation up.

"It sure teaches you a lot about yourself."

Yes, I want to tell him. It already has. But that would be profane, because Ted's voice has become soft and confiding, and I have to admit, just for a moment, a flare of curiosity arcs in my brain. What did it teach him?

"Good night, Ted," I say. "And thanks."

# CHAPTER 4

I'M SQUEEZING ALEX'S mortal ass, fucking her from behind, my fingers in her mouth. She bites on my fingertips and then sucks. A finger of sweat inches down my concave chest toward her Murray Hill behind. I'm out of breath.

Up to now, this kind of ass, this kind of body, would have been entirely out of reach. Even my father, who slept with all those women, probably never had this kind of sex.

"Don't come," she says, grabbing my balls from underneath and squeezing them just hard enough so that I get the message. She turns around, my cock still in her, and smiles at me, a piece of her brown hair pasted to her forehead. She's caught in a trapezoid of sunlight, her skin burning white. I have to blink and focus again. Behind us, I can hear the clacking of the hanging blinds that separate the bedroom from the balcony.

"Let's take a break," I say, slipping out of her. "Have a cigarette or something."

"I think I'm going to have to find another cancer stud," she says, rolling onto her side, one hand resting on her thigh. She rests her elbow on the king-size bed, her cheek in her hand. As I turn to the beveled mirror above the dresser, I can see her considering me. I pull on my boxers and pants, take her husband's mono-grammed silver shoe horn, and wiggle into my tas-seled loafers, which I wear only on special occasions. Unfortunately, I made the mistake of exploring their walk-in closets when she was in the bathroom, and his shoes alone put me to shame. Fine grained, blacker than black. Wingtips. Oxfords. All custom-made. His fitted shirts draped in dry cleaner shrouds. A silver box filled with gold cuff links. And lurking in the corner, a bag of expensive-looking golf clubs. Without even meeting him, I was getting an inferiority complex.

And yet, here I am, sweat still cooling on my face and chest, framed in the enormous mirror above their dresser.

Alex is pulling open the balcony's sliding glass door.

"You're naked," I say.

"Who cares?" she says, stepping outside. I join her there, still buttoning my shirt. Her ashtray and cigarettes sit on the concrete floor. As she lights up, I lean over the railing a half foot and take in the view.

The tarpaper buckling on the tops of the older build-
ings. The sun smeared on the face of a skyscraper. The
thickening traffic on the FDR Drive, and beyond that
the whorls of the East River, flashing back at us.

Alex is standing next to me now, narrowing her eyes
against the glare. Elbows pinning her breasts together
against the slight chill. A rash of goose pimples appear
on her thighs, arms, and calves. Suddenly, she waves.
And looking in that direction, far away, on another con-
dominium ledge, I see a tiny blot of white wave back.

"Is that a guy?" I say.

"I think so," she says.

The blot sits back down on a chair on his balcony
and continues to stare. I wonder how many of these
other tiny people there are, between jobs, retired,
home from school, peering at us through the slats of
Venetian blinds, or pulling Alex into focus behind the
lens of a Stargazer telescope, thinking: What is she
doing with that guy?

"He probably thinks I'm some rich nymphoma-
niac," Alex says, exhaling as she speaks, the smoke
instantly ripped away. Up here, the wind gusts make
mincemeat of human emissions.

"Maybe he's dying, too," I say, trying to make her
feel better.

"We're all dying," she says. "We just got to skip a
few grades."

"Did your tests come back?"

Skipping a few grades is fine, but I don't want Alex to graduate early. I really don't want her to die.

"They did."

"And?"

"Early acceptance," she says.

"What about chemo?"

"Useless. They're already talking about palliative care. And here I am, just standing here. Feeling totally normal."

"It sucks," I say. "I don't know what to say."

"You don't have to say anything," she says. " 'Cause you know how it feels."

She tosses the cigarette and turns to me. Her body is a bigger liar than I am. The blue veins just visible under her perfect, slightly small breasts. The sunlight lacing her trimmed pubic hairs. The muscular dent in the side of her thigh when she shifts her weight. Her graceful neck. All the bad news she's been getting seems purely hypothetical to me. A bunch of opaque, relentlessly specific pages in a manila folder on her desk, labeled by Alex, almost off-handedly, CANCER STUFF.

"You get your second wind?" she says.

I follow her back into the bedroom, glancing over my shoulder one more time at the guy on the other balcony. He's waving at me, very slowly, his barely visible hand tocking back and forth like a metronome.

• • •

Alex says it's time to squeeze a life of luxury into every living day. She's got her husband's platinum Visa card. Now that I'm on leave from work, I'm free to follow her around all day. We hit Barneys and she buys me a two-thousand-dollar buffalo-hide biker jacket and a thousand-dollar pair of shiny black boots. We fly through Bergdorf. She buys a sable coat and almost leaves it behind at the store café. I sip cappuccino at the salon while she gets her hair done, then she makes Rex cut mine. It's the most stylish haircut I've ever had, with a little fringe on the bangs, a mop effect on top. Alex looks even better. Less Murray Hill, more Upper East Side. Her brown hair cut short and straightened. A new black pearl necklace fastened around her neck. But each time her husband's credit card is swiped, she looks a little less satisfied, and by the time we push through the revolving doors of Bulgari, she's completely lost interest.

"I'm tired," she says. "Let's get something to eat."

We take a walk through Central Park along the pond. It's getting dark earlier; the lamps have already been turned on, dead leaves heaped against the wrought iron bases. We sit on a bench, and because it's starting to get cold, Alex pulls her hand away from mine and retracts her fingers into the cuffs of her fur coat. She looks transfixed, staring at a curtain of algae on the surface of the water, already glistening in the artificial light.

"Isn't it incredible?" she says.

"I love the fall," I say, playing with the zipper of my new leather jacket. I smell like a very expensive barn.

"No. The fact that we're not going to be here anymore. That this is all going to go on without us."

"But we'll still be here," I say, trying to reassure her. "Even the warmth of our bodies is generating energy right now. Who knows how long those molecules might last."

Alex is shaking her head slowly.

"No," Alex says. "This is it. You know the funny thing?"

"What?"

"Last week, before this happened, I thought I was the center of the universe. I didn't tell anyone I was. It just kind of felt that way. And then suddenly the world's not even paying attention to me. That's how we die. Just like that."

Now I'm getting depressed. I wish she'd get back on track. What happened to living a life of luxury in a day?

But by the time we walk to Columbus Circle and take the elevator up to Per Se, Alex is irretrievably depressed. At a table that's big enough for ten people, we stare, not at each other, but through the plate-glass window at the lights in Central Park, aircraft blinking over Fifth Avenue. Seventeen infinitesimal dishes are brought to us, and I gorge on each one, realizing I'll probably never eat like this again. Alex eats only a few beads of caviar. It's like the most expensive lousy date in the world.

"Alex," I say gently, touching a warm oyster with my spoon. "You've got to try this."

"I'm not hungry," she says. Her necklace gleams under the lighting. Slavishly prepared plates are accumulating in front of her like jewels, and all she can do is look out the window. It isn't until we get to dessert that she comes alive.

"Double espresso," she says to the waiter with a smile.

"The same," I say.

"I don't want to sleep tonight," Alex says to me. "I don't want to waste any more time. I've got to figure out what I'm going to do with the rest of my life. We could still do something amazing."

"Learn to hang glide or something," I say.

"Fuck that," she says, squeezing my wrist so tightly that blood beats in my fingers. "We could become human bombs or something. Blow up Bush."

"I'll think about it," I whisper, with a frozen smile on my face, glancing to my left to see if any of the waiters have heard. I lift up the leather cover of the dessert menu, wondering if there's any chance I can order a fifty-dollar glass of Calvados. When I look up again, Alex is standing up. She tosses me her husband's credit card.

"Keep it," she says. "I've got to get out of here."

Thursday afternoon. Squirrels defying gravity on the fire escape, jerking their tails. The distant sound of a power saw. I've been watching daytime television while waiting for Alex to call me back. It's a beautiful afternoon in late October, and I should be lying in her monstrously large bed, or watching her stretch, naked, on her balcony.

"Alex," I say into the phone when her voice mail beeps. "Where are you? I'm getting worried. All that bomb talk. Anyway, I'm still here. Sitting at home. Call me?"

An hour later, still no call. Instead, the keys in the door. Lee walks in, wearing her charcoal gray business suit and white stockings, ringlets of blond hair tucked behind her ears. Leaning over the easy chair, she kisses me on top of my head.

"I can't get over that haircut," she says. "You look totally different."

"It's just a haircut," I say. But the truth is, I feel different, too. I feel like I did before I met Lee. I'm a bachelor again. The only problem is, I'm sitting in a married guy's apartment.

"Is this a good time to talk?" Lee says, sitting on the couch as I restlessly change channels on the television.

"You've got to see this *Oprah* highlight," I say. "Did you know the twentieth anniversary of her show is coming up?"

These are the details only a man with serious cancer knows.

"Paul," Lee says. "Turn the television off."

"She gets snubbed at this French designer store and then she gets payback. I watched the whole thing this morning."

There's a rustle of static and then the television screen goes black. Lee puts the remote down and looks at me sadly.

"You're watching *Oprah and Oprah* highlights?"

"I have cancer," I say angrily. "That's what we do. We distract ourselves."

Lee sits down on the couch and pins her hands between her knees. She tilts her head slightly.

"I think it's nice you got a haircut, Paul. I think that's great. And the leather jacket. And the boots. I mean, if I had cancer, I'd go on a spending spree, too."

Her whole face lights up, as if someone had just tugged the chain of the sympathy bulb. I'm waiting for the *but*.

"But," I say, unable to withstand the silence.

"I feel like you're starting to act a little strangely."

"And," I say.

"I want the old you back."

I know exactly what *that* means.

"This is about getting you pregnant, right?" I say.

"Can't we talk about it?"

"No," I shout. "How can we? I'm not going to be around in five years. Possibly three."

"Stop talking like that," she says, her face flushing. "Sometimes I think you just want to die."

I peel myself out of the leather chair and sit down next to my wife. I put my arm around her shoulders and pull her closer. I hadn't expected this. I thought that the first mention of having serious cancer would rule out the kid thing forever. We'd glide right over those child-bearing years, by which time her mother's ashes would be scattered over Lake Fingerfuck or whatever cold body of water in which she wanted to be dissipated, and we'd collect the two million. Then we could talk about that five percent survival rate all she wanted. I'd be a walking miracle.

But the thought of having a kid, the need to have a kid. It's a little like cancer. There's always the threat it's going to spread. I'd have to handle it very carefully.

"My mother wants us to go on vacation," Lee says, staring straight ahead.

"That's really big of her," I say. For someone worth

millions, Lee's mother keeps her wealth close to her chest. This threadbare Oriental rug under my black boot, that's all we'd gotten this year, and it was something she'd obviously wanted to get rid of.

"She wants to pay for it."

All right, I think. Now we're getting somewhere.

"That would be wonderful," I say. "Someplace low key."

"I could take a week off. I mean, this time between us is so precious now."

I pull her close again. I peck at her coils of blond hair.

"I think," I say, "I should go by myself."

Lee pulls back and stares at me in a funny way, as if some bug were slithering across my face.

"By yourself?" she says. "I don't understand."

"This might be the last time I really get to figure out who I am," I say. "Really get to the bottom of me. I'm going to need to concentrate."

"All right," she says softly. "I guess. Like a retreat or something?"

"Sure," I say, turning on the television again. "Like St. Croix. Or St. John. There's this killer beach there called Cinnamon Bay. I saw it on the Travel Channel."

Although I'm trying not to notice it, Lee is giving me a long look.

"Jesus Christ," I say, grabbing my shoulder and leaning over.

"What?" she says, throwing her arms around me.

"Sudden pain." I say. "Terrible pain."

"I'll get one of my Vicodins," Lee says, standing up.

"No," I say, leaning back on the couch again. "There. It's gone."

Lee's giving me another long look, but it's a sweet one this time.

"I'll call my mother today. It's a good idea. You deserve it, Paul. You've been really incredible."

I am incredible. I do incredible things. With my new fringy haircut and buffalo-hide jacket, I'm the Cancer Cad.

Tonight, the lovely Terfins have invited us over. Brenda's a stay-at-home mom. Felipe is her lawyer husband. I've always liked Brenda. She's a little pixie, with an upturned nose and a Betty Boop haircut. But she's never flirted with me once. The second Lee and I walk into their narrow duplex apartment, that all changes.

"You look great," Brenda says.

"Doesn't he?" Lee says, flicking back a strand of hair near my ear with her finger. It's a territorial gesture, but Brenda doesn't back off. Instead she takes my hand and gives me a long, sincere look.

"Lee told me about the cancer," she says.

"You did?" I say, turning to Lee with a slightly scornful look. This is working out perfectly.

"I needed to talk to someone," Lee says.

"We're really sorry," Felipe says.

Brenda's husband is not bad-looking—solid chin, well built, naturally confident—but the new Paul seems to throw him off balance.

"It's actually been a blessing," I say in an almost holy voice, gripping Felipe's hand. I read that somewhere and liked it. And it really does the trick now. Brenda's eyes are glazing over with emotion. Felipe's usually strong handshake seems to evaporate in my fingers, and he slinks away to the kitchen. Brenda, on the other hand, just keeps on staring at me, as if I walked in with monkey-sized angels on my shoulders. And I know why Brenda is looking at me. As hip and lovely as she is, she confided to Lee that she's a born-again Christian.

"That's such a beautiful thought," she says.

"It really throws everything into a whole new light."

At the mention of the word *light*, Brenda's eyes widen, as I knew they would. Born-again Christians just can't deal with that word. It's like catnip. They want to roll in it like kittens.

"I want to know more," she whispers to me, smiling, as we walk to the table and take our seats.

Felipe gives his wife an angry look. I decide it's better to stick to the usual mundane subjects at dinner. No point in making the poor guy even more jealous.

After we pass around the blackened tilapia, we talk about the Park Slope Food Coop.

"You know what I hate?" I say, eating with gusto. "They freeze all their hamburger meat."

Felipe and my wife are looking at me with expectant eyes, waiting to see if this is all I've got. But looking at Brenda, I realize it's more than enough.

"I hate that, too!" she shouts.

"Brenda," Felipe says, his thick eyebrows scowling downward, jerking his chin at his two-year-old daughter reading behind us on the couch. "Justine's having quiet time."

So Brenda just smiles at me as I finish the last of my tilapia.

"Have more," she says, lifting up a plate that's the shape of a giant spinach leaf.

"I thought we were keeping the rest for tomorrow," Felipe says.

"Don't waste it on us," Lee says, giving me a nervous look. "Got to save room for dessert. Right, Paul?"

Sure, in the old days, I used to save room. I saved room for sex, for food, for relaxation. I became a mansion of saved rooms. Now, I gorge on everything. Felipe watches in astonishment as I scrape the last of the tilapia off the spinach leaf, then take the tiny pink bowl containing the mango salsa and empty the last of it over the fish.

"I'm going to finish reading Justine her book," Felipe says angrily. Back in the days I was just me, a mumbling bore, Felipe had no trouble drawing the conversation away from me. I always left their house starving.

"I'll clear some of this stuff off the table," Lee says, pushing back her chair. I smile at Lee politely, but Brenda doesn't say anything. Hands neatly folded under her chin, she's watching me eat.

"It's delicious, Brenda," I say. "What did you do to this?"

"You squirt some juice on it," she says. "Let it soak in."

Felipe has raised his head from the pages of *Curious George*. I smile politely at him to show that I have no ulterior motive.

"That must be so hard," Brenda says admiringly. "Just smiling. Or sitting here and listening to the same old conversation. I'd be manic."

It's true. I endured and partook in their boring conversation. And now there will have to be atonement. I set my death-ray eyes on full power and lower them toward Brenda.

"When the time comes," I say in a deeper voice, "I think you'll do fine."

As Brenda's eyes and mouth widen again, I find myself wondering, Do I have room for two? Alex and Brenda, and even perhaps a third? Will I keep a brown leatherbound book like my father's and in precise, tiny handwriting note the date, time of day, and place? Could I break six hundred?

Under the oak table, I link hands with Brenda, our fingers braiding themselves together as we listen to Felipe tell Justine about the man in the yellow hat.

She's scraping my palm with the nail of her forefinger, crossing the equator of my life line, digging playfully into my wrist. If the old me could just see me now! It feels like her hand is making love to mine.

"You were flirting with her," Lee says, when we're alone together in the Mazda, the heater doing its best to melt the frost on the windshield.

"Of course I was flirting with her," I say. "I'm dying. And dying people don't always act rationally."

Lee's face looks older under the jaundiced glare of the overhead lamp. There are a few stray hairs on the shoulders of her jacket. Pouches under her eyes. Her left hand, which fidgets with the latch of the glove compartment, is roped with veins. And I know what you're thinking. It's on the tip of your tongue.

She looks old.

But I don't stoop that low. I love my wife. I've just chosen to take advantage of a once-in-a-lifetime opportunity.

"What about me?" Lee says. "I know what you're going through is terrible, but what about my feelings?"

"Did you even read the brochure I brought back from the doctor's office?"

"Yes," she says softly.

"The part about anger, denial, and acceptance?"

"I did."

"Well," I say. "I still haven't reached denial. So you're going to have to be patient. Some cancer patients die before they even get to acceptance."

Lee opens her mouth to say something, but turns toward the window instead, where some man in a tan trenchcoat is standing over his squatting golden retriever, balanced on all four legs like some canine lunar module.

I let down the emergency brake and put the Mazda in first.

"Paul," Lee says. "I'm almost afraid to ask you this."

"Shoot," I say.

"I don't understand why you seem so happy."

"Typical reaction to a grave diagnosis," I say. "At any moment I could crash. Literally. Feel suicidal and drive right into another car."

"Okay," Lee says nervously. "I won't ask you any more questions."

*Cancer,* I'm thinking as I grin for no good reason. *Where have you been all my life?*

• • •

Yes, you say. This is where he pushed it too far. Doing the hand dance with Brenda Terfin while her husband read *Curious George*. Lying to long-suffering Lee in the Mazda.

Fine, I'll skip the following day. Meeting Brenda in the playground. I had the time, didn't I? Walking home slowly with her as she pushed the baby stroller, dead leaves scraping under our feet, the first pumpkins appearing on stoops. I'll skip the charade we made of having actual tea, her daughter finally drifting off to sleep. Brenda didn't even bother taking her out of her carriage. She led me upstairs, to the alcove, kicked aside a baby yoga book, and placed one slightly cold hand inside my shirt, asking me softly, Where is it? I'll skip all the cancerous places I pointed to, places she then kissed. I'll skip the way she tucked her naked knees into the spaces behind my legs as we listened to her baby daughter talk in her sleep. I'll skip all this because I want to get to the part of my day I really want to skip.

Alex committed suicide. Jumped off her balcony. I wasn't there. The doorman, eyeing me very warily, told me about it when I showed up later that night.

There, it's done with. Saw it coming. Terrible thing. Let's move on.

Shall we?

# CHAPTER 5

TWO WEEKS LATER, on a cold November morning, I left for Cinnamon Bay. I mean, I began the first stage of my journey to that crescent-shaped paradise. I drove the Mazda to Kennedy Airport, by way of the Belt Parkway, admiring the thickening clouds over the Verrazano-Narrows Bridge, the glowering river. Storm coming in, and lucky me, I was escaping. Put the car in long-term parking, slung my duffel bag over my shoulder, and walked through a very bright corridor of glass, the tail section of a United Airlines jet moving sharklike along the blast fence.

I feel like I'm on a business trip, but the wonderful thing is I'm working for myself, and what we're working for twenty-four hours a day is unalloyed pleasure.

Unslinging my bag I take a seat on a stool in the Crow's Nest. It's not even ten o'clock in the morning and I'm ordering a giant mug of beer. Through the slanted plate-glass windows I watch a jet drag itself into the sky, distorted by its own vapors. The bartender is wearing several large buttons, some with smiley faces, some with dire warnings. She's in her twenties. Soured by all this light and motion. The stink of those eggs drifting over from the Farmhouse Café.

"Sweetheart," I say. "Would you slide me that bowl of mixed nuts?"

"Slide it yourself," she says.

Should I pull out the stops? Tell her this is my last vacation? Tell her this is the last monolithic beer I'll probably ever have in an airport bar? No, not worth it. I lean over and grab the mixed nuts.

"I want to sit at the bar," someone says behind me. I turn and see two people. One, a very attractive, full-figured blonde holding some androgynous, stuffed pink horse, and standing next to her, about hip-high, a kid wearing a Minnesota Vikings cap, maybe seven or eight years old. He has piercing brown eyes, and before I can even turn away, he's hopped up on the stool next to me and he's piercing them at me.

"Are you an alcoholic?" he says.

"Excuse him," his mother or guardian or stuffed animal carrier says. She's wearing a silky white blouse and black skirt, with a thin gold necklace around her neck.

She squeezes the back of his neck playfully, but he wrenches himself away and continues to stare at me.

"I asked you a question," he says.

"No," I say. "I'm just having an early-morning beer."

The truth is, I'm terrible when it comes to talking with kids. It's a no-win situation. You talk to them like adults and they just end up asking you embarrassing questions. You try talking to them on their level and you end up looking like a closet pedophile. I avoid talking to them at all. Like this, I turn my head, pretend to be interested in another takeoff. Fortunately, the bartender has noticed the little brat, too.

"You can't sit at the bar. The bar is for grownups."

I continue to stare out at airplanes, waiting for the sound of his little feet as they go shuffling off, but all I hear is the sound of his cap being placed on the bar.

"Oh," the bartender says. "I'm sorry."

"No reason to be sorry," the other woman says. "We can move to that table over there."

"No," the bartender says. "Just make yourself at home. What do you want, honey? A Coke? A ginger ale?"

I have to turn to see what all the fuss is about. The kid is completely bald. Leukemia probably. Sitting there like God's gift. Taking his sweet time to decide between soft drinks.

"Coke on the rocks," he says, staring at me again.

The blonde hops up on the seat next to him. Now we're all in a row, sitting at a nearly empty bar, an invisible cloud of bacon grease wafting in. I know what I have to do. I have to preempt him. Ask him some silly question that'll throw him off my scent. Or something so boring he'll just leave me alone. Because he's still looking at me.

"So where are you headed?" I say, nervously twisting my giant beer.

The tone of my voice seems to instantly annoy him.

"Mom," he says. "Can you move down one seat?"

"Why?" she says, punctuating his rudeness with a quick smile.

He motions for her to come closer so he can whisper. His hands megaphoned around his mouth.

"Because," he hisses so loudly that the bartender whips around, "he's really creepy."

"It's okay," I say, standing up. "I need a little more space anyway."

I bring my beer and the bowl of mixed nuts to one of the small laminated tables and sit down. The clouds that had been thickening over the Belt Parkway are now moving across the runway and the light has turned yellow and strange. A couple of floppy birds near the runway tower seem lit from within, two bright specks flapping into the noxious black. I'm watching them fly upward when a flash of lightning seems to rise up from the ground. And then another.

"Shit," I say out loud, looking at my watch. I don't want to be delayed. In six hours, tops, I've promised myself I'm going to be sitting at the swim-up bar in St. John's, a thatch of brown leaves gently stirring over my head, some charred British bombshell next to me, spellbound by the story of my last voyage.

But these are my lucky days, the days I only dreamed of when I was so busy being a mewling nice guy. And that's why I hear my flight being called. My ribcage expands with happiness again. I suck in a lungful of eggs and bacon grease, giving the mother of that bald brat a pitying look.

"Good luck," I say, winking once.

This is what I'm doing when the ticket agent's voice comes over the loudspeaker and announces that my flight to St. John has been cancelled. I'm looking at a brochure of the Caneel Bay Resort, reading all about The Self Centre, which helps guests realize their own desires through a variety of mind and body approaches.

"Flight 384 to St. John," her voice says, "has been cancelled because of a mechanical problem."

I crumple the brochure into a tight ball and jam it into my pocket. I'm not the first passenger to crowd around the ticket desk, but when I finally get my turn, I'm the most furious.

"So what flight do you propose to put us on?" I say grandly, looking around at my fellow frustrated passengers, who have begun to drift away. Hang in there, I want to tell them, You don't know the power of terminal cancer.

"There's another flight tomorrow at five forty-five in the morning," she says, punching a few keys on her computer. "I can put you on that if you like."

"This is unacceptable," I say, looking for support, but only an elderly couple remains, the husband repeating the necessary facts for his hearing-impaired wife.

"I don't know what to say," the ticket agent says.

"I am terminally ill," I say gravely. "I do not have a day to waste."

"My wife is, too," the husband croaks, nodding his head in sympathy and pointing to his spouse.

"What?" his wife says.

"He just said he's terminally ill," her husband croaks into her ear. "He doesn't have time for this."

"Good for you," his wife shouts. "What do you have?"

"Cancer," I shout back.

"Liver failure," she says.

"I can put you on a flight to Minneapolis," the ticket agent says nervously. "And you can connect there. I'm very sorry, but it's the best I can do."

"Minneapolis?" I say.

"I can upgrade you to first class."

"It's a *thousand miles* in the wrong direction."

"It's the best I can do, sir."

But I'm already walking away, so indignant that I'm cursing out loud. Although, somewhere in the back of my head, where my primitive impulses meet actual thoughts, a voice says:

Wait. Think about this. You don't actually have a terminal illness, remember?

Maybe it's a bit out of the way, but you'll arrive in St. John sometime tonight, and dine barefoot on lobster. Walk home arm in arm with two deliciously drunk Aussies by the light of leaning tiki torches.

Go to Minneapolis.

Me, Mrs. Liver Failure, and her doting husband are the last passengers to board the flight to Minneapolis/St. Paul. We struggle down the aisle like penitents, glared at by our fellow passengers. Fortunately, since we've been assigned seats in first class, there isn't very far for us to go. Still in a daze, I flop down in my seat, and immediately realize that this can't be right.

I'm sitting next to that brat, who's still wearing the Minnesota Vikings cap, still piercing me with those brown eyes. I'm thinking of the ticket agent. How I told her I had a terminal illness. The little do-gooder probably thought it would be a great idea to stick me and the kid together. Idiot, I want to tell her now, cancer doesn't have any father figures. Especially father figures who are lying to begin with.

"Mom," he says to the blonde I winked at an hour ago, "I want to change seats."

"We can't change seats, Jack," she says patiently. "The plane is starting to move."

"Your mother's right," I say, pulling that brochure out of my trouser pocket. "You could fall over and kill yourself. We wouldn't want that."

Uncrumpling the brochure, I spread it out on my lap and turn to the page I was looking at, dimly aware that Jack is reading along with me.

"What's a Self Centre?" he asks.

"It's a place that grownups go to pamper themselves."

"Sounds gay. Is that a picture of it?"

"Yes," I say, looking at the airy room with the picture windows facing the sea. Fluffy canvas pillows strewn around a darkly stained floor.

"Don't bother the man, Jack," his mother says. "He's trying to read."

"He's not reading," Jack says. "He's looking at some stupid picture."

"Jack."

"All right, Mom."

And with that, Jack turns away and goes back to violently playing his Gameboy. Despite the occasional intrusion of his pointy elbow whenever he scores a touchdown, despite the unnecessary gurgles he has to emit as he guides his virtual players around the postage-stamp-sized screen, I fall, somehow, asleep, and dream for some time before another hand, a grownup hand, grasps me around the wrist.

I stare up into the face of Mrs. Liver Failure's husband.

"Good for you," he says, patting me on the wrist. "For speaking up. And I'm very sorry to hear about your cancer. We'll see you in St. John."

"Thank you," I say as he drifts away with a conciliatory smile, wiping some sleep spit off my chin with the back of my hand, and letting my eyes close again.

"You have cancer?" Jack says.

I am patient, even as we travel in the wrong direction at 550 miles an hour. I am patient and listen to Jack talk about his leukemia. I had just begun to explain how my cancer had leaped to my lymph nodes, mostly for the benefit of his very good-looking mother, when Jack abruptly cut me off.

"That's nothing," he says, tearing off his cap again, patting his own head. "You still got your hair."

"My cancer is different," I say. "You can't treat it with chemotherapy. It's a skin thing."

"Must not be too serious if your hair hasn't fallen out. My doctor says he doesn't even know how I do it.

He thinks I'm some kind of hero or something. I don't know about that though. I'm just a kid."

"I'll probably die before you," I say.

"What?" he says, terror brimming in his eyes.

"*Excuse* me," his mother says, her expression completely changed. She looks like she's ready to smack me.

"I'm not going to *die*, stupid," he says. "What are you talking about?"

"I meant I'm a lot older than you," I say, trying to recover. "You're just a kid."

"Right," he says, giving me a long look. "You want to see my autographed photo of Demetrius Davenport?"

Yes, I think, let's change the subject, because obviously I'm not in my usual groove today. Think of this stretch of time as something that will be deleted from your mind as soon as you touch down in St. John, I tell myself. Like a selected block of text on a computer, just *deleted*.

But why is that name so familiar? I ask myself, as Jack reaches into the back of the seat and retrieves a special folder with his name written on the front in Magic Marker. He opens it proudly and hands me an autographed photograph of Demetrius, the same photo I had seen in *ESPN Magazine* while I was in the waiting room, sitting a foot away from Alex Hivinshki. Demetrius, half naked and indestructible, hands on hips, looking righteously pissed, and then a thin scrawl of handwriting on the bottom, probably written by some lackey.

*To J,*

*Hang in there tough guy.*

*D*

The guy didn't even have the time to write out his full name. Or Jack's.

"Cool," I say, handing the slick photo back to Jack, who very carefully puts it back in his folder.

"I'm going to see him," Jack says. "In Minneapolis."

"The Wish-on-a-Star Foundation put it together," his mother says. As she tells me this, I get a better look at her face. Not pudgy exactly, but full. Probably a knockout in college, married some barrelhead, then this happened and it's probably all she can think of. Except for a little lipstick and eyeliner, she's not madeup. But her eyes are as blue as my missing ocean, and there's a weariness about her that would have appealed to me in my former life, when I identified with anybody who looked slightly worn out.

I don't miss that guy at all. But there are times I feel like he's trying to make a comeback. For instance, flying to St. John by way of Minneapolis is something my old self would have done.

"It's going to be great," Jack says, staring out at the wing.

"Don't get your hopes too high," his mother says.

"I'm Paul," I say to her, reaching across the aisle.

"Barb," she says, letting her fingers fall away as soon as I've grasped them.

# CHAPTER 6

THE DREADED FIVE-HOUR layover. What's worse? Too long to be wandering around some airport. But yet too short to escape into the nearby city. It's a state of droning indecision. As I exit the flight, having done my best to say warm good-byes to Barb and Jack, I slip into the nearest bathroom and relieve myself.

"Sir," someone says to me as I walk away from the urinal. "We flush here."

"I thought it was automatic," I say, walking contritely back and slapping the lever with my hand.

But even after I walk to the sink and hit the pump faucet with the heel of my hand, my error is still being discussed out loud by the man standing at the urinal.

"I just believe in accountability," he mutters. "And everywhere I travel, I just notice it. This lack of moral principles. Sure, he's just walking away from a urinal. But it's probably the tip of the iceberg."

And that would hold some water, it really would. But he's talking to himself. There's no one standing next to him. He's crazy.

I shoulder my duffel bag and walk out of the bathroom, waving as Barb and Jack pass by.

"Why don't you come with us?" Jack says.

"He can't," Barb says. "He's got to catch another flight."

"Five hours," I say. "I guess I'll hit the game room."

I can hear the canned noise from where I'm standing, the sudden defibrillation of some fun-filled machine.

"It's not too far from the airport," Barb says. "You could probably make it back and still have time to be bored out of your mind."

"There's going to be cheerleaders," Jack says. "What's the drama?"

"Listen to you," Barb says to him, in an admonishing voice.

But Jack's right. What is the drama? I tell myself. And a lot could happen in five hours. You and Barb could end up somewhere alone. It's possible.

"All right," I say, catching up to them. "What's this guy's nickname again?"

"Demetrius 'the Hurt' Davenport," Jack says.

"That's a horrible nickname," I say, feeling a little deflated. But then I remember that interview in *ESPN*

*Magazine*, and what the bullies in school used to call Demetrius.

"What are you smiling about?" Jack says.

"Nothing," I say. "Can't a man smile for no reason?"

The Twin Cities Boys and Girls Youth Recreational Center is a narrow three-story brick building pinned between a church and a Laundromat. Ordinarily, you could probably walk right in, grab your recreated kid, and walk out. But today, two vans from the local television stations are parked outside, their satellite antennas already raised, and a clutch of about fifty people are arguing with a large white security guy, who's yelling something into his miniature cell phone. The cab we've taken from the airport is idling down the street, our bags sitting in the trunk. Barb has a whole itinerary in her pocketbook. Apparently, the Wish-on-a-Star Foundation has scheduled Jack's entire day, including naptime, but the *Dream Lunch with Football Superstar Demetrius Davenport* is the only thing that Jack really cares about. And after quickly glancing at the rest of Jack's itinerary, wondering when I might get to spend a little grownup time with his mother, I realize how terribly organized this Wish-on-a-Star day is. Why the three-hour block of time set aside for Foosball, for instance? Couldn't they have come up with something better than that for kids who have precious little time to begin with?

There are four hours and fifteen minutes until my flight to St. John departs, and I let out a shallow sigh, realizing it might have been far less painful if I had stayed in the airport game room, or cranked my chin up in the gate area and watched *Headline News*.

"Hold my hand," Barb says, grabbing Jack's fist and pulling him toward the blocked entrance. She's holding the Minnesota Vikings football that Jack wants Demetrius to sign in her other hand. I follow a few feet behind, watching Barb gently pat the backs of the men and women crowded in front of her, who only dart her annoyed looks. It's Jack who knows just what to do.

He takes off his cap and pulls down the corners of his mouth.

This seems to set off an instant chain reaction. A woman notices first, then a man, then another man, and pretty soon the whole crowd is parting in front of him.

"Are you coming?" Jack says, looking back toward me.

I nod and follow humbly. The three of us stand in front of the white guy with the cell phone, who flips a page on his clipboard and asks for our last name.

"Volero," Barb says, one hand on Jack's shoulder.

"Don't see it," the man says, flipping another page.

"Maybe they spelled it with a *B*, Mom," Jack says.

"No Bolero here either," the man says.

"Well, you're going to have to let us in. You can call the Wish-on-a-Star Foundation. We've come all the way from Rhode Island."

"I can't call anyone right now, Miss," the man says, "I'm providing security."

Barb nods at him, as if she understood perfectly, and then pushes right past him. It takes two more security guards almost five minutes to push Jack and Barb back outside the building. I, of course, do the obvious. I watch the fracas and look at my watch. Exactly four hours till my flight leaves. It's just one of those days that starts out wrong and keeps on going, and someone's going to have to put a stop to it.

"Thanks for helping," Barb says, shaking out her sleeves, then looking over her shoulder. "Is it ripped?"

"A little," I say, touching the back of her jacket. Jack, I notice, is clutching his mother's pocketbook, which got torn off in the struggle. He's staring back at the security force hatefully, as if staring alone could do the trick. But it doesn't. The men go back to talking into their mouthpieces and pushing back other fans, and Jack begins to cry.

"Hey," I say, patting the top of his head, but it's too late, fluid is running out of every hole in Jack's face except for his ears. And then he does something that

catches me by surprise. He grabs the hem of my buffalo-hide leather jacket, the centerpiece of my travel-
ing-in-style outfit, and wipes his face on it.

"I'm sorry," Barb says, covering her mouth. Moth-
ers are always secretly delighted when their child's
bodily fluids happen to someone else.

"It's okay," I say, raising the hem to get a better look
at the map of snot covering the side pocket. Jack sniffs
and stares up at me with red-rimmed eyes. His face
is so puffy it looks like he's had some kind of allergic
reaction.

I pat him on the head again, and wonder, at the
same time, why I'm doing this. Please stop, I tell myself.
You look ridiculous. Please get your fucking bags out
of the trunk of that cab and find another cab and tell
that driver to get you to the fucking airport.

But instead I play catch. Right on that sidewalk.
Tossing Jack's unsigned Minnesota Vikings football
back and forth, doing my best to achieve something
better than a wobbly spiral. When Jack drops the ball
and goes running after it, I look at my watch again.

Three hours and forty five minutes.

"Do you believe this?" Barb says, staring at her cell
phone in exasperation. "They put me on hold."

She's sitting on a stoop, my mucked-up jacket
hanging neatly over the wrought-iron railing.

"Run a pattern," Jack says, cocking his arm back. I

mime a square out, holding out one hand, realizing at the same time that Demetrius Davenport has emerged from the entrance of the building. I hear the actual screams of his fans before I see his shoulders riding above the crowd. Jack's already running toward him, with the football in his hand.

A black Cadillac Escalade pulls up to the curb. Demetrius's fans have formed an instant double line that leads all the way to the open passenger door. But Jack, manic now, has thrust between them and Demetrius nearly trips over him.

"Get this kid out of my way," he says to one of his security guards. I have just enough time to register that fact that he looks the same in person. Arrogant eyes. Broad cheekbones. A diamond stud in his ear.

"I'm Jack Volero," Jack says. "The Wish-on-a-Star Foundation said you wanted to meet me."

I'm pushing through the line as well now, but less successfully. Someone elbows me back.

"I'm done signing," Demetrius says, pushing the football away. "Get out of my face."

"He's telling you the truth," I shout. "He came all the way from Rhode Island."

"See how this works," Demetrius says, shaking his head at one of his security guys. "Daddy just turns around and sells it."

"I'm not his daddy," I say, but my voice is sucked

up by the requests of other fans. I can't see Jack anymore, just that stupid unsigned football bouncing above people's extended hands, and then the football isn't even there anymore. Demetrius Davenport rips it out of Jack's hand and throws an eighty-yard Hail Mary that everyone turns and follows. It's the most beautiful, cruel, tight spiral that was ever thrown to no one. And it lands with a loud thunk on the hood of our waiting taxi. The driver, who had been asleep, wakes up in horror, stares for exactly one second at the enthralled crowd looking at him, and drives away, our bags still in the trunk.

In a state of shock, I look at my watch one more time, and am reminded of those frozen timepieces after the blast in Hiroshima. Three and a half hours to go.

"I'm fucked," I say softly.

"Oh *shit*," one of the fans says.

"Look at his face," someone else offers.

When I turn around, I see Demetrius smiling at me, one shiny shoe already planted on the running board of the Escalade. His brown eyes searching mine, quite confident I don't have a trace of pride left.

"Have a nice day," I say. "Pig-eye."

Behind a thin curtain, in the ICU of Fairview Hospital, I dangle my blue cotton booties and wait, touching the seven blue stitches on the bridge of my broken nose. Novocaine coats the back of my throat and I still feel pretty charged up, though my caved-in septum has already been pushed out by the surgeon, with an implement that looked a lot like an ordinary teaspoon.

"Hey," Barb says, pushing back the curtain.

"Heyffn," I say, through the gauze in my nostrils, the aluminum splint on my nose vibrating.

There's something very tender and alarming about seeing your own sorry condition reflected in another person's face. A mirror I can deal with. Two black eyes. An unrecognizable nose. Fine. Next case. But Barb looks like she's walked into the wrong movie. A tear-jerker about a guy who sticks up for a kid with leukemia and ends up having his nose shattered by a narcissistic wide receiver. As she gently rubs the back of my hospital gown, which, for some reason, is covered with tiny teddy bears, I want to tell her it was the disappearing taxi that made me snap. At least let me have that. The old me. That guy who wasted so much of his life pretending to be nice, watching Lisa Hunt swallow her pills and thanking her for that lousy hot chocolate coffee, is never coming back. You can break my nose a hundred times.

I'm not going to end up like my brother.

And besides, it's four forty-five according to that clock on the wall. I have fifty minutes to get to the airport.

"What are you doing?" Barb says as I stand up,

rip my bloody clothes out of a transparent plastic bag labeled *biohazard* and start putting them on. A minute later, I'm fully dressed. I must look like a chainsawed extra in a horror movie. Blood on my white shirt. Blood on the cuffs of my designer jeans. Blood on my argyle socks. My new Frye zip-up boots, bless them, have, for the most part, escaped. Just a little splatter effect near the toe, which I scrape off with my fingernail. I'll go shopping when I get to St. John. Besides, all I really need is a bathing suit there anyway.

"Airport," I say, patting my back pocket to make sure the wallet is still there.

"Your plane left hours ago," Barb says.

"It's not even five," I say, pointing to the clock.

"It's not moving."

And she's right, the sweep hand is stuck. I'm stuck. I've been stuck since that little shit walked into the bar at JFK.

"Why is this happening to me?" I yell at her, snatching the rest of the curtain back, which reveals my neighbor, an elderly man covered up to his neck with a gray blanket, two tubes forking out of his nose.

"Jesus Christ," he says, staring at me, pressing the nurse button on his handrail.

"It's okay," I say, holding up my hand. "I'm a victim, too."

# CHAPTER 7

I HATE EATING with children. I imagine it with fear whenever Lee brings up having kids. First of all, they're at least four years old before their little beady eyes break the plane of the table, and then you have to endure ten years of inane conversation that would make someone with ADD look like a genius. It's all about *them,* and yet, they have nothing to *say.* Even the abandoned peas on their tiny plates start to shrivel with boredom.

But here I am, in the dining room of the Minneapolis Millennium, thickly carpeted and heavily chandeliered, listening to Jack talk about my broken nose.

"Your eyes are going to be black and blue tomorrow," he says. "We're going to have to buy some raw meat and you're going to have to tie it to your face. Right, Mom?"

"I think that's an old wives' tale," Barb says, sawing gently into some chicken cordon bleu.

I deliberately ignore Jack and flick two pecans off the top of my baked salmon. Typical overreaching menu. The dreadful feeling that I am mired in someone else's sense of bad taste. Look at this plate: the initials of the hotel traced on the rim in wasabi and lime ink. I should be in St. John right about now, and my heart aches because I can feel myself landing, the double thump of the landing gear. The staircase pushed up to the plane. The warm, perfumed air. Waiting cabdrivers in white shirtsleeves.

"You probably won't ever look the same," Jack says, leaning over to sip from the straw connected to his ginger ale.

"Jack!" Barb says, glaring at him. She's still wearing the silk blouse she started the day with. And there's a noticeable run in one of her glossy white stockings. I like to think it was caused by her running toward me after I was knocked out.

"I have to prepare him," Jack says solemnly.

I delicately put down my fork and touch the adhesive tape X'd on the bridge of my nose. When I touch my nose, the back of my skull aches. It makes no sense. Neither does this hastily purchased wardrobe. At six in the evening in Minneapolis, the only clothes I could find were at a sports souvenir shop, and what's worse, the only jersey they had in my size was Demetrius Davenport's. Yes, I'm wearing number 78. I paid forty-three dollars for the privilege of wearing my attacker's purple jersey. And I've capped this off with a pair of purple-and-gold leisure pants that tear away at the sides. Though I insisted on wearing my boots to dinner.

"Thank you for preparing me, Jack," I say. "You are truly wise beyond your years."

I raise my glass, already drunk on the combination of Vicodin and cheap Yellowtail Cabernet. Yellowtail! Presented to us as if it were some ancient bottle of champagne.

Jack raises his ginger ale, oblivious to my sarcasm. Barb, giving me a sort of affectionately cross look, clinks her wine goblet to mine.

"A toast," I say, letting my hand linger in the air, where the glass catches the track lighting just so, and makes my head hurt all over again. "A toast to Jack's unsigned football. A toast to our missing luggage. A toast to the painkillers I swallowed an hour ago and that are just kicking in."

I clink both their glasses again and swallow the rest of the wine. Jack rests his glass on the table and sucks his straw, looking at me intently.

"Now Barb," I say. "If you don't mind giving me the room key, I think I'm going to head upstairs before I pass out."

"He's sleeping with us?" Jack shouts.

A pale white couple, both wearing gunmetal glasses, swivel their heads around and stare at me.

"Just one night, Jack," Barb says.

"Why?"

"Because he stuck up for you. Because he's a nice guy."

*Nice guy.*

I push back the chair and stand up. And then I'm on my way, my heels sinking into the elaborate curlicues on the carpet, my leisure wear gleaming. In the many-mirrored elevator, I squint and read a placard advertising an ice-fishing expedition, stumble out on the fifth floor, and insert the room card into the slot. My bloody clothes have been neatly folded by the maid and set on the luggage rack. And outside, that storm that seems to have followed me all the way from Brooklyn is finally coughing up some precipitation. Thin flakes of snow, spinning around the window. I'm already lying crosswise on the bed, staring at my hazy reflection in the cataract of the television screen, listening to a couple chatter in the hallway. Only vaguely, as I finally pass out, do I realize that they're talking about me.

"Did you see his face?" the man says.

"How about his clothes?" says the woman. "And we thought San Diego was too casual."

"This is our brave new world," he says, fumbling with the card. "Heaven help us."

• • •

What I have always dreaded is the thought of one day waking up to the sound of cartoons. But when you're headed in the wrong direction, the things you dread have a way of finding you.

I wake up to the sound of a Ping-Pong championship game on ESPN 2. Someone has taken my boots off. Someone has carefully laid a blanket over me. Barb is sleeping on the other bed, wearing the MINNESNOWDA T-shirt she purchased yesterday at the souvenir shop.

It's strange to wake up in a hotel room with a woman you haven't slept with. It's strange because we've known each other exactly one day, and to be honest, if I knew me for one day, I wouldn't fall asleep in the same room.

"Who took off my boots?" I mumble to Jack, who's sitting in front of the television cross-legged, as if it were a glowing fire, his back against the bed.

"Mom did," he says sourly, without looking at me. Clearly, I've thrown a wrench into his oedipal plans. His Wish-on-a-Star fortnight away from Dad, back in Rhode Island.

For some reason, I find the image of my boots being dragged off by Barb tender and fascinating. I want more information.

"One by one, or both at the same time?"

Jack, unfortunately, doesn't even attempt to answer

this question, so I'm left to invent the scene myself. I see her hands pulling off one boot at a time, then laying the blanket over me.

"I can't believe this is the only thing on," Jack says. "I hate Ping-Pong."

Picking up the remote control, he flicks at mind-numbing speed through the channels, stopping momentarily at a Doppler radar map of the Minneapolis/St. Paul area, which for some reason is completely covered in green. I get out of bed, still wearing my leisure pants, and pull back one of the curtains.

"Holy shit," I say.

The balcony. The parking lot. The median. The cloverleaf. Everything has been erased by fresh snow.

"I know," Jack says excitedly, leaping up and joining me at the window. "It's going to be a megastorm. They say we might get up to sixteen inches."

I look down at the shiny top of his bald head, at all the lumps and tiny bumps on his small skull. For a moment, I feel like I'm looking at some charming alien, who just happens to be occupying the same hotel room as I am. Then I touch the bandage on my nose and wince in pain, just to remind myself about my lack of judgment yesterday. This, in general, is where sympathy leaves you. Snowbound in Minneapolis. Staring out at a culvert. Or an embankment. Or whatever lies beneath that mound of snow near the highway. It looks like I don't have to worry about having kids, because I'm already trapped with one.

"Let's order room service," Jack says, grabbing the laminated menu off the floor. He's probably been reading it for hours, deciding on hotcakes with bacon, then French toast, then hotcakes with sausage, and back again. He hands it to me and then begins whispering manipulative, sugary good-mornings into his mother's ear, covering her cheek with ulterior kisses.

"I'm sleeping," she says.

"Get up," Jack says, pulling the sheet back. She sits up and reaches for it, but he's dragged it off the bed. Rubbing her eyes, she smiles at me, then looks out the window.

"It's snowing," she says, catching her own excitement, as all grownups do when it comes to freak weather. You have to inject a little disappointment.

"I know," Jack says, grinning in the same direction. "We're going to be stuck here for days."

"I should call my wife," I say, after the orange juice has been drunk, after the cold scrambled eggs have been eaten, after the cold toast has been crumbled.

Jack, of course, like all kids, is about one sixteenth of the way through his meal. The thrill of his expectation matched by the tediousness of the actual eating. Barb is trying to butter an oat bran muffin that instantly comes apart in her hand. Of course, she knows I'm married. She must have seen the ring. But we haven't really had time to talk about any of that. Jack had been too busy interjecting himself into everything.

Since my cell phone is in my duffel bag, I really don't have any choice but to use the room phone. As I pick it up, I wonder whether Lee has been trying to call me, and imagine my cell phone ringing in the trunk of that escaped taxi.

"It's me," I say, when she answers.

"Hi," Lee says, in a far less friendly voice then I expected.

"I'm not in St. John."

"You're not? Where are you?"

"Minneapolis," I say, staring at Barb, who is whispering something to Jack, doing her best to pretend she's not interested in my conversation.

"I don't understand," Lee says.

"It's a long story. They gave me a voucher for this hotel room. And now it's snowing. A lot."

"No," Jack says loudly.

"Who was that?" Lee says.

"Some kid," I say, glaring at him.

"In your room?"

"No," I say, scrambling. "He's in the hallway. The maid's got the door propped open with her mop bucket thing."

"He's *lying,* Mom," Jack whispers.

Barb presses one finger against her lips and gives me a concerned look.

"She wants to vacuum," I say, partly covering the phone to address the imaginary maid. "One moment, please. I'm on the phone with my wife. Lee, I'm going to have to call you back."

"Tell her to wait."

"I can't," I say. "They're very pushy here. I'll call you back later."

"I need to talk to you," Lee says ominously as I hang up.

I'm still looking in the direction of the invisible maid, and then I gaze imploringly at Jack and Barb. *Listen,* I want to tell them. *It would be impossible to explain.* But the guilt I feel is short-lived, because Barb takes the phone from my hand and dials home as well. And her conversation is even more shameless.

"I'm checking in," she begins, in a clipped voice. "He's fine."

Barb turns her back to us, and I smile at Jack, just in case he has any ideas about telling his father what's really going on. But Jack couldn't care less. He glances at me once and then stares back down at his food. Now that his breakfast has failed to live up to his expectations, he has decided to torture it, spilling five containers of fake maple syrup on his leftover hotcakes, then impaling the dough with two crispy shards of bacon.

"I'm not going to get into that with you again," Barb says. "The answer is no. Tony, drop it. Besides, I'm here with someone. Yeah, a guy."

Then I can actually hear a human voice violently demanding information on the other end. But Barb is holding the phone up in the air, shaking her head, mouthing the word *psycho* before she drops the phone back in its cradle.

"All *right,*" she says, walking back to the table. "Now that *that's* behind us."

I watch her put her arm around Jack's neck and pull him toward her, gently strangling him.

"Stop," he says with delight. "Can we stay here, Mom?"

"Sure," she says, smiling back at me.

"I'm serious," Jack says.

Jack wants to take a bath. Behind the bathroom door, Barb and I listen to him splash water, his flesh squeaking against the back of the flimsy tub.

I take another sip of my pale orange juice. There's something about this heavy silverware, the dull light on the plates, the finger of fluffy snow on the railing of the balcony, the sound of Jack's voice as he talks to himself in the bathroom, and Barb and I sitting here watching the weather. It all throws me for a loop, and I don't know why. I have a broken nose. Some dirty surgical tape is coming off my right nostril. I missed my flight. And this is definitely the wrong place. Isn't it?

"So that was your husband," I say, wiping my upper lip with the back of my hand.

"Ex," Barb says. "I can't get rid of him. He uses Jack to stay in my life."

"One of those," I say, nodding knowingly.

"Jack can't stand him either. He's just one of those people. I had no idea what he was really like when I married him."

"I know what you mean," I say. "Once you peel the layers away."

"*Layer,*" she says. "Underneath he's just this jealous psycho. And if you ran into him, you'd think he was the most normal guy in the world."

"You're divorced?"

"It's still in the works. With Jack's leukemia, I haven't even had the time to finalize it. And this year hasn't been good. It really hasn't been good."

She places her fingers on her eyebrow and tries to gather herself. She doesn't want to cry in front of me. She doesn't even know me. And what can I say? What can I do but tilt this three-holed stainless steel salt shaker and wait for the turbulence to pass?

"Jack's not doing too well," she whispers. But my "sorry" never makes it out of my throat.

"I need a towel," Jack shouts from the bathroom.

"Get it yourself," Barb shouts, safely back in present-tense mother-mode. "I'm not your maid."

"Nice attitude," Jack says.

"He's completely spoiled," she says softly. "If he were healthy, he wouldn't get away with any of this. But you know. I just want to give him everything. I never want to say no."

"Sure," I say, knowingly. "And he's taking advantage."

"Did you ever?" she says haltingly. "Use your illness. You know."

"There have been times," I say, as snow is blown against the balcony door like sand, "that I've been tempted."

"Well," she says. "You sound like a nice guy. On the phone with your wife, I mean. Besides."

"Besides?"

"You're a terrible liar."

Showered, freshly dressed in our same old clothes, the family that really isn't heads down to the hotel lobby, where the clerk, surrounded by more track lighting and teak, informs us that Demetrius Davenport would like us to be his guests for the day and that he's waiting for us outside.

"I'm calling the police," I say.

"I'll handle this," Barb says, furious. "Watch Jack."

"Barb," I say, as she marches through the lobby, ready to give Demetrius a piece of her mind. I should be the one racing to meet him. But all I can do is put my hand on Jack's shoulder.

"What if he hits my mom?" Jack says, looking up at me.

"I think he's just making a courtesy call," I say, trying my best to look reassuring. But Jack wriggles his shoulder from my hand and runs after Barb.

Good, I tell myself. Let them go. Just let them.

But I'm picturing that Hail Mary pass, the one that led to my broken nose. And suddenly I'm so pissed that I'm spinning through the revolving doors. Bursting outside, I see that Barb is already jabbing her fingers into Demetrius's chest. Three security guards, one white, two black, stand back with their hands clasped, and I get the feeling that Demetrius has ordered them to be on their best behavior. But when they see me, decked out in Demetrius's jersey and still wearing the same boots, they can't stay straight-faced.

"Shut the fuck up," Demetrius orders, and they listen. I'm standing under the overhang, my wet hair warmed by a battery of heat lamps, realizing I've just made another mistake. What I should do is turn around, run through the lobby until I find a suitable potted plant, and hide. I don't want to be Demetrius

Davenport's guest. I want to be sitting cross-legged at the Self Centre, inhaling ylang-ylang.

"Look at his face," I hear Barb say.

But she doesn't have to tell Demetrius, because he's already looking at me in amazement. He's shaking his head at me like a long lost brother.

"You take a pretty good poke," he says, spreading his fur-clad arms. I cower under his incredible wingspan, feeling the soft fur descend on my ears. The diamond stud in his ear indenting my forehead. I try to hug him and feel even more feminine, my hands slipping under, and not over, the massive fur coat. With the heat lamps still burning above me, with my humiliated blood boiling within, I feel like I'm trapped in some kind of incubator.

"Let go," I hear Barb say, and one of Demetrius's arms is tugged away. "He's had enough. You're just scared because you think he's going to sue you."

"Demetrius Davenport screwed up," Demetrius says, shaking his head at me. "And now he's here to make amends."

"Well Paul Mauro is fucking *livid*," I say, noticing that Jack is climbing into the Escalade, the white security guard with the goatee dutifully holding the door open for him.

"Livid?" Demetrius says with a shrug. "Help me out."

"Pissed off," I say. "Furious. Filled with rage."

"Got you," Demetrius says, noticeably relieved. "We can work with that."

"Get out of that car, right *now*," Barb shouts at Jack.

But Jack is already lost in the shadows of the Escalade. A DVD screen has been pulled down by another lackey. An Xbox joystick handed to the smiling child.

"Relax," Demetrius says. "He's having fun. Let's all have some fun. Troy, show this lovely couple to the car."

# CHAPTER 8

SOMEWHERE OUTSIDE OF the Twin Cities, there are snow-covered fields, and distant pines, and frozen lakes, and small black dots here and there, bent over holes in the ice.

"They fishing," Demetrius says, keeping one thumb on the wheel but turning toward the backseat, where I sit with Barb and Jack. The white guy with the goatee and ridiculously large shoulders is staring out his window at the distant shapes as well.

"Nothing like it," the white guy says. "Cut a hole in the ice and just spend some time with yourself."

"I still don't understand that," Demetrius says, flooring the accelerator. "Demetrius can't sit in one place. He doesn't want to stare at some hole in the fucking ice."

"Watch your language," Barb says fiercely, squeezing Jack's hand. But Jack is no longer with us. He's playing Crackdown on the Xbox, his chin raised high, eyes reflecting another massive explosion.

"One day I'm going to drag your ass out there," the white guy says. "Serious. You've got to try it."

"No," Demetrius says, stepping harder on the accelerator until he's almost riding the bumper of the black SUV in front of him, where the rest of his crew ride. "I prefer this. Snowmobiling."

I watch what's left of my visible face in the rearview mirror. I look concerned. Two black bruises deepening under my eyes.

I'm going too fast to really be angry anymore. A Kawasaki Thundercat pinned between my legs, a rooster tail of blue snow arcing behind. It's amazing how fast these machines actually go, I'm thinking as I race back to the treeline again, my helmet buffeted by a blast of icy wind. Demetrius is just ahead of me, bent forward on his snowmobile as we explode up another virgin trail, a flock of birds tossing themselves up from the bare trees.

Parallel to Demetrius, I lift my visor and we both slow down.

"This is great," I say. "The thing *moves*."

"Can't hear you," he says.

"We're going really fast," I shout.

Demetrius winks at me and points ahead, where the

trail opens up into a giant clearing, bigger than a hundred football fields, painted a warm, glowing yellow by the noonday sun. Yes, my nose was broken by this man. And no, this isn't St. John. But am I really so far off course? Am I having a kid? I'm living the bachelor life with a football star, and later, who knows? Cigars, charred steaks, top-shelf tequila, celebrity golf.

As I pass Demetrius, I lean all the way to one side of the snowmobile and bob my helmet.

"What the hell is that?" I hear him shout.

"The gangstah-lean," I say. "What does it look like?"

"That's good," he says. "That's really good. You want to race?"

And we do, eighty miles an hour, all the way to the far end of the bowl, where, quite suddenly, my engine cuts out. I come to a slow, crunching stop. There's nothing quite as deflating as being the master of the wilderness, taking acres of it in almost off-handedly, and then suddenly becoming *part* of the wilderness. Two tracks behind me. Two feet of icy crud in front of the still-warm engine. Fortunately, Demetrius is right behind me. I wave to him with my flexible leather glove, rings of rubber sheathing each knuckle. My fingers are already getting cold.

"What happened?" he says. "You just stopped."

"Fuck," I say, turning the key. I don't want to be stopped. I want to keep going, gliding, tearing up virgin forest, disturbing the eternal birds. This is the kind of fun I've been waiting for all my thirty-eight years. If my brother could just see this.

"Let out the choke," he says.

I do this, and turn the key again. There is a brief burble from the engine, and then nothing. The sound of a tree creaking. Demetrius moving in his parka. Our breath entangling.

"You know what I think," Demetrius says. "I think you ran out of gas."

"I doubt that," I say, with a hint of doubt. "I mean, your guys topped off our tanks before we left. Right?"

"My guy topped off my tank. I don't know what your guy did."

It hits me before it hits me. He's going to leave me out here. It was all planned. He's already turned his ignition key. He's throttling up. Okay, I get it. He's still a little sore.

"Demetrius," I shout. "I read it in some magazine. In a waiting room. I didn't mean it."

With each statement, his snowmobile pulls further away. But then he circles back and glides slowly by me.

"I'm going to freeze to death," I say.

"Go for it," Demetrius says, giving me the thumbs-up.

"Why are you doing this?"

" 'Cause I broke your nose, man."

He clucks once as if this logic should already be obvious.

"You're going to leave me out here to die because you broke my nose?"

"Lawsuit," Demetrius says. "Can't afford one more. I'm already paying out of my ass for the shit that went down on that party boat."

"I won't sue," I say. "I promise."

"Put yourself in my position," he says. "Would you take that chance?"

"I have cancer," I shout, but Demetrius is gunning the throttle again, turning the steering bar. He can't hear a word. The tread of the Thundercat kicks a few handfuls of snow on my visor, and he's gone. A minute later he's crossed the clearing, where the snow has already formed a thicker layer of crust. How many miles did we drive? I frantically try to figure it out. But it must have been at least thirty, and I don't remember seeing a single sign of civilization. And for the first time in my life, I know I'm really going to die. Like Alex knew she was going to die.

If I'd never picked up that stupid magazine in the waiting room, if I'd never read that dumb interview, I'd never be here.

No, you asshole, I tell myself. If you hadn't lied. If you hadn't lied you wouldn't be here. You'd be back in Brooklyn getting Lee pregnant, and it would still be better than this, wouldn't it? Shivering on a snowmobile.

• • •

At some point darkness actually falls. But I'm so busy having an imaginary conversation with my brother on his back porch in New Jersey that it hardly matters to me.

"Can you turn on the light?" I say to him, taking the joint from his hand.

"Who needs the light?" he says, lifting his chin. "We got the moon."

And he's right. Over there. Huge and preciously yellow. Hovering over South Orange.

"I lied to Lee," I tell him, handing the joint back. "I told her I had serious cancer."

"You have serious cancer?"

"I just told you. I lied. Actually it's more like an exaggeration."

"Why?"

"I don't want to have kids. I don't want to be *you*."

"That's nice, baby brother. That's heart-warming."

"Come on, Eric," I say, leaning back on the railing. "Admit it. You've been trying to kill yourself for years. You're miserable."

"You're never going to get it, are you?" he says, tossing the roach into the same old pile of dead leaves. "There's love here."

"Don't start with that again," I say, surprised that one of the dead leaves is actually burning a little.

"You got a glimpse," he says. "Didn't you?"

"When?" I say, noticing another leaf catch fire. Just enough flame now to heat your hand.

"When you stuck up for that kid. That's how it all starts. They get this helpless look in their eyes. That's why we had three kids. Each time they looked a little helpless I wanted them to have more company."

"The leaves are on fire," I tell him, in a detached sort of way.

"I know," he says. "It's all part of the plan."

"What plan?" I say.

"You'll see," he says, reaching for his beer bottle and opening the screen door. I start to follow him, but then I decide I should watch the leaves burn, just in case it gets out of control. A spark could land on the house, set the roof ablaze. I dust a glowing bit of leaf off my shoulder. It's getting so hot that I take off my parka, then my T-shirt. I tell myself there's no fire, no brother, that I'm miles away from New Jersey and that it must be five below, out here in the middle of nowhere, the yellow skin already frozen off the moon. It reveals itself for the cold-hearted bastard it really is, shining cold silver on my naked shoulders.

On the horizon, through distant trees, I can see two needles of light, then four. And gradually, the purr of snowmobiles moving toward me. I wave my arm as best I can, the frozen snow around me turned lunar by the headlamps. The engines die down and I can make out the sound of muffled laughter. And then a long, giddy pause.

"We just fucking with you," Demetrius says. "Get on."

I collapse on the seat and hug his parka. Demetrius peels away first, leading us back from where we came. But I'm still staring back at my brother, who's waving to me as the leaves burn.

"We have to go back," I say, wondering why Demetrius can't see the conflagration. The house that's about to go up in flames. My brother and his family are inside. I don't know if he set the fire on purpose or by mistake, but we have to save them. For once, I think I understand. How Eric could love his family and want to destroy it, and how each emotion only makes the other stronger. My father was the same way. And me, I just opted out before it got ugly.

"The house is going to catch fire," I shout at Demetrius, slapping his back as he drives across the icy field. "We can't leave them."

# CHAPTER 9

BACK IN THE hotel room, under two blankets, I feel like my core body temperature is still twenty degrees below normal. Barb has cranked up the heat but it only makes me feel like a rapidly dissolving ice cube in a bowl of hot soup.

Of course, Jack thinks if it weren't for him, I'd be dead. As if being the victim of Demetrius's cruel practical joke isn't enough humiliation, I now have to deal with the fact that Jack thinks he saved me.

"I get to stay up as late as I want tonight," Jack says. He's sitting at the foot of the other bed, watching television.

"And why do you get to do that?" Barb says.

"Because Demetrius asked me if he should go back and find him, and I said 'yes.' And if I said 'no,' he'd still be out there. He'd be dead."

"Jack," Barb says, sitting down next to me. "It's

not nice to brag like that. And he's still not out of the woods."

"I'm sure my survival instincts would've kicked in," I say. You'd think that freezing to death would make me really see the light. But the only revelation I'm having is that a frozen man's penis is the first part of his body that thaws out. It rises majestically under the sheet and gently asks me what Barb is doing in the other bed.

"Jack started to cry, you know," Barb says. "When we were waiting for Demetrius to find you."

"No, I didn't," Jack says.

I lift my head off the pillow and take another sip of the lukewarm tea that Barb brought me.

"We can still call the police," Barb says.

"I think I've had enough excitement for the day," I say. "Maybe we just turn off that television. Isn't it past Jack's bedtime?"

"I'm not tired, Mom," Jack says. "And besides, it's been a really stressful day. I need to unwind."

"I'm not going to argue with you, Jack," Barb says, grabbing the remote out of his hand. Jack glowers at the blank screen, eyebrows leveled above his brown eyes.

"Did you really cry?" I ask him. I want to know what he looked like when he started to cry, the same way I wanted to know how Barb took off my boots when I was sleeping. Some of the best moments are those we're not there for, when, by sheer grace, and by the tiniest thread, people keep us in mind.

Jack doesn't answer but his silence says everything. That much I know about kids. They tell you everything when they aren't speaking.

"Well," Barb says. "Here we all are again."

"Stuck," Jack says, only faintly pleased by this notion now. He hadn't banked on his mother's tenderness toward me. The teacup hovering near my lips.

I blow some steam away and sip again.

"When I wake up," Jack says angrily, "we're going to Tiny Town."

Jack finally falls asleep, next to his mother, in the other bed.

"You're still trembling," Barb says, her fingers on the switch of the bedside lamp.

"First the cancer," I say, making my voice sound shaky. "Now this. I guess somebody up there just has it in for me."

"I could lie next to you," she whispers. "It might help."

Barb switches off the lamp and crosses over to my bed, her body traced by moonlight, or a floodlight, I'm not sure which.

"Are you sure he's asleep?" I say.

"Out cold."

The next step is a cinch. My cold hands seeking warmth under her shirt. My cold lips on hers. Her thick blond hair falling over my face. She sweeps it back with her hand. Kisses me again.

"Oh my God," she whispers.

"What?" I say, kneading her ass with my fingers.

"Your hands are like freezer packs."

"I'm sorry," I say.

Barb's reaching through the elastic of my boxers, searching for evidence of genitalia.

"There you go," she says. "Poor guy."

I've never had sex with a child sleeping in the next bed. It's a stop-motion film. A thrust, a groan, and then three seconds of holding your breath. It feels like we're trying to do two things at once. But sooner or later, sex always wins. We stop stopping. We make a little noise.

"Mommy," Jack says, reaching dreamily for her absent shape.

"It's okay," Barb says to me. "He's still asleep."

She's on top of me now, rocking back and forth over my chilly thighs. If Jack wakes up and looks over at us now, he might be scarred for life. Though it might take him a few minutes to figure out what's happening under this tent of comforter and sheet.

"Don't come inside me," Barb whispers.

"I don't have to come at all," I say, magnanimously.

"No, go ahead," she says, lowering her hips again.

"I want you to come," I say.

"I can't," she whispers. "I don't want to make too much noise. You come. It's all right. Just come. Come all over my ass."

"Mommy."

"He's asleep. Keep on going."

"I'm not asleep, Mommy. I'm wide awake."

And Jack is. He's lying on his side, looking right at us. Probably wishing he never cried back there in the woods. Because the only one who's getting the royal treatment is Paul Mauro.

"Mommy was just making Paul warmer," Barb says, flopping on her back. I grab the remote and turn on the television, furrowing one eyebrow as if I had been watching this movie all along.

"Paul's warmer," I say, holding her hand under the sheet. "Paul feels terrific."

And I *do* feel terrific. Barb sleeps next to me. Jack seemingly buys our explanation and falls asleep, too. But for some reason, I wake up at six, just as a clear blue sky is lightening the moldy drapes, and I can't get back to sleep.

I think: I want to keep on going. One direction always. And see how far I can keep on going. Because the old me, he could only dream of that.

I think: This strange happiness I'm feeling is just

the excitement of uncertainty. And people make mistakes when they're uncertain. A mother makes love to me while her child tries to sleep in the next bed. I almost buy it in a snowy field, and suddenly these two strangers think they're responsible for me.

I think: I am not responsible for them.

I think: Look at her face. The tiny spot of dark drool on the corner of the pillow. Her pink nail polish. Her strong jaw. Aren't her eyes a little too small? And him, hidden under his sheet, barricaded by pillows, in love with her more than you'll ever be.

I think: Leave them. Leave them and move on. You don't need another family. You just narrowly avoided one. You *hate* kids.

I dress like a thief. I put on Demetrius Davenport's football jersey. I snap the buttons of my silky leisure pants behind the closed door of the bathroom. I zip up my boots, and I leave the bloody shirt and pants behind.

I would have kissed them both, I swear I would have, if I could have been certain it wouldn't have woken them up.

An hour later I'm at the airport.

In retrospect, I would have to say that the game room at the Minneapolis-St. Paul International Airport was not the smartest place to be two hours before my flight left for St. John. I have both hands on the steering wheel of a video game called Roger Roadkill when I hear my name being shouted over the racket. No, I think. That can't be Jack's voice. Jack is back at the Millennium with Barb. And I'm here, just trying to kill the last few hours I'll ever spend in Minnesota.

"Paul," Jack says, grabbing my arm. "I knew we'd find you here."

I smile at him and look up. Standing just outside the game room, Barb glares back at me, a carry-on bag around her shoulder. She's wearing a brand-new pair of jeans and her battle-scarred tan jacket. And the first thing I realize is that I'm happy to see her, despite the expression on her face.

"Come here, Jack," Barb says. "We've got to find our gate."

"I want to play Roadkill."

"I'm not fooling around," Barb says, walking into the game room and grabbing Jack's elbow.

"Get off," Jack says. "I want to hang out with Paul."

"I didn't want to wake you guys," I tell Barb. "I should have left a note or something. I'm sorry."

"I'm really glad you didn't freeze to death," Barb says. "The world would have lost a really great guy. Ten minutes, Jack. I'll be at the newsstand."

And then she turns to me, blue eyes patiently waiting for me to look at her directly.

"I can trust you to watch him for ten minutes. Or are you going to run away?"

"Barb," I say, but she's already turned her back.

"You made her cry," Jack says. "Give me a dollar."

I take out my wallet and extract a dollar, which Jack feeds the video game.

"I didn't know you guys were leaving today," I say.

"Dad called Mom and made a big stink about visitation," Jack says. "We have to go back."

For a few minutes we drive our separate cars over a succession of pixellated rabbits, skunks, and deer, veering off the road in billowing clouds of dust. When the game ends, I look around to make sure no one is looking, and then I get on one knee.

"Jack," I say, putting one hand on his shoulder and looking at him earnestly. "I want to thank you for yesterday. I'm alive because of you. I would have frozen out there."

"How come you left without saying good-bye?"

"I don't know. I should have. Can I say good-bye now?"

"No," Jack says. "Give me another dollar."

We feed the last of my dollars into the machine and run over more woodland creatures, avoiding the occasional hitchhiker and crossing guard. It's a gory game no good parent would ever play with their child, but I'm not a parent.

"You got a high score," I say to him, twisting the wheel until the first three letters of Jack's name are entered.

"It's missing a *K*," Jack says.

"We only get three letters," I say, grabbing his hand and leading him to the door.

"Let go," he says. "I'm not a baby."

Sulking, he lags behind, fingering every coin slot, pressing his nose against the Plexiglas case filled with stuffed animals.

"It's a ripoff," I say, mostly because I feel bad I don't have a dollar left.

"I know," he says. "I have enough stuffed animals anyway. They just sit there."

We find Barb at the newsstand, flipping through the pages of *Celebrity Weekly*. She glances up, frowns at me, and tosses the magazine back on its stack.

"What gate are you at?" I say.

"8A," she says. "You?"

"I'm down on the other concourse. I had some time to waste."

Halfway down that long green corridor, at the start of the walk-o-lator, we hug each other, or try to. Barb stays stiff as I clasp her shoulders, and Jack goes completely limp, as kids do, letting one slightly cold hand sit on the back of my neck.

"I'll come visit," I say, as they step on the moving walkway and begin to get smaller.

"I know you will," Jack says with a confident grin. Barb has already turned away, but her son looks at me until we can't see each other anymore.

"Right," I say sarcastically, when he's out of earshot. Much as I like the kid, the last place on earth I'm going to be visiting is Rhode Island. Cross that state off my list, too. It's definitely not part of the straight-line plan.

That's that, I tell myself, walking toward my gate with growing excitement. A new, blank page has been turned. I'm tossing my keys and wallet in a gray plastic bucket. I'm taking off my shoes. The metal detector beeps once and a tiny light goes green.

Finally, I tell myself, as my boarding pass is ripped and handed back to me. I'm headed in the right direction.

# CHAPTER 10

I AM STANDING in four feet of the clearest water known to man, making circles on the surface with my fingers. The water is hugging the crotch of my palm-frond bathing trunks and I don't even have to wince.

The temperature is perfect.

The sky is perfect. Just a few slowly moving clouds, way out there on the horizon, where the cruise ships slide by.

The sand at my feet is perfect. No sharp rocks. No pebbles. No sea urchins. As perfect as the sand on the beach, which is raked every afternoon by a team of men in white uniforms, like some infield crew.

The moon and the sun are perfect, and both are visible in the sky. The moon playing dutiful backup to the burning superstar. Holding the roses, taking the calls, calling the car.

And there isn't a child in sight. They're taken away

here, led to hidden playgrounds or underground grottoes by the Caneel Bay staff. Once or twice, I thought I could discern a childlike scream in the distance, but that was it. The noise was quickly extinguished.

My broken nose is even looking better. I took off the bandages today. There's just a little yellowish black bruise left under each eye.

I have finally arrived at exactly the place I want to be, so forgive me if I stand here for an extra minute or two, smiling goofily at the flat sea, tracing these thoughtful circles with my fingers.

I'm brilliant. I really am. Don't I deserve a little credit? I know, I know. A late-bloomer, but still. I could be sitting in Englewood Cliffs next to Lisa Hunt, watching her unscrew her pill bottles. I could have a fucking kid!

I could even be dead. Frozen solid on the back of a snowmobile. But when you have a little momentum, nothing really gets in your way, not even cancer. And I still have that, by the way. Just in case I meet the right person here.

I breathe deeply, pretend that my lungs are two burlap bags, as the yoga instructor said. I breathe this impeccable air and crouch until the water reaches the tiny hairs on my shoulders.

In the afternoon, a group meets at the Self Centre. After a short lecture in a large room, cantilevered over the rocks, so that it appears we are floating over the sea, we are sent to private rooms, where we exchange our clothes for flowing robes. We reassemble outside, shaking hands and exchanging pleasantries. Looking down at the folds of my garment, I feel a little like Jesus. We *all* look a little like Jesus. Even that woman with the halo of gray hair. Even that short, balding man.

We begin our BreathWalk, following our leader, a very fit Austrian named Jurgis. We walk single file along a narrow white path, through clattering palms and bent green grass. For every step, as ordered, we take one breath, exhaling as soon as our bare heels hit the ground. The circular path is completely devoid of obstruction, raked by the same grounds crew that takes care of the beach, but there is one tiny hill. A ladder of four smooth rocks, one breath for each, and then you're back on track. Here, the group bunches up. The lady with the gray hair is taking a little extra time, and I take this opportunity to talk to the pretty woman with the auburn hair and mysteriously curved nose.

"Amazing up here, isn't it?" I say.

"No talking please," Jurgis says. "It's not in the spirit of the BreathWalk."

The woman with the curved nose looks at me sheepishly and continues on. No big deal, I tell myself, I'll catch up to her later.

• • •

My BreathWalk is followed by a long massage. There is the heavy smell of eucalyptus. A perfectly folded towel lies across my ass. I'm not allowed to talk here either. I can only watch as Brice, a broad-shouldered Australian with his black hair tied in back, clasps another sizzling pancake-sized rock with a pair of giant tongs and gently lowers it on my spine. I cringe.

The process is repeated until I have seven large rocks on my back. Ordinarily, I would find this funny. Ordinarily, I would say something. But whenever I start to emit a sound, Brice places his forefinger against his lips.

"Feels great," I say, breaking the rules.

Brice sighs loudly and places the last rock on my back. Does he really take himself this seriously? What's wrong with a little small talk? Finally, I'm in control of my life, and I wind up on an island populated by transplanted control freaks.

No, Brice doesn't say anything till the end of our session, when he gives me a funny look.

"What happened to your face?" he says.

"Oh," I say. "I did a little ice climbing out in Minnesota. I slipped."

"I teach a self defense course in the afternoon," he says. "We meet over by the paddle boats."

"Thanks," I say politely, backing out of the eucalyptus-filled chamber. Another activity, just what I need.

Me and my fellow vacationers aiming slow motion kicks at the gently lapping sea.

I dine by myself. The waiter is friendly enough, but even when I ask him about the flavor notes of the wine I'm enjoying he shakes his head good-naturedly. He doesn't speak English. So all I can do is pretend to be interested in the old lobster traps and pockmarked buoys that hang under the thatched roof and flirt with the girl with the curved nose. She's dining alone, too, but instead of walking across the sand and introducing myself, I decide to wait for the Singles Jamboree.

"Another glass of wine," I say, lifting up my empty goblet as the waiter passes. I need to get a little more sauced before I'm ready for the limbo, but they're already lighting the tiki torches along the pathways. I can already see myself walking back to my whitewashed stucco bungalow with the curved nose, ocean rippling sleepily in the distance.

"Shhhh," the very friendly staff member in the straw hat says.

"Sorry," I say.

I'm standing in the center of the circle, although it's not much of a circle. It turns out there are far fewer singles at Caneel Bay than I had first thought. The prettier women all have husbands and Aryan-looking kids. The rest of us get to play charades in front of this bonfire. Awful, unimaginative charades. The lady with the gray hair has already pretended she was some kind of shark. The short bald guy stood on one leg and flapped his arm behind him until we all gave up. And now it's my turn.

I look at the girl with the curved nose, and I know, despite all this silence, that we're still going to end up together.

But now, it's first things first. I have to make the most of this.

I make a C with the fingers of my left hand. I make a sad face. I begin digging up imaginary earth.

"Treasure," the bald man shouts.

I shake my head. Patiently begin again. The C. The sad face. More imaginary earth thrown in the air. Then I clasp my hands together in prayer.

"Church," the gray-haired woman says.

I sigh deeply, and doing so, realize that I am looking up at the stars.

I point up and then drop down to the sand on all fours, doing my best to imitate a crab.

"Cancer," the bald guy shouts.

I give him the thumbs-up.

"That's great," someone says, and there's congratulatory laughter until everyone notices the stricken expression on my face.

"Oh," the girl with the curved nose says, pressing her long fingers against her mouth, her crimson fingernails gleaming in the firelight. And I know I have her.

The old me would never have had sex with a blinking light going off on the phone beside him. The old me would never have had sex like this, period. Curved nose's name is Lucy and she's from Dayton. No, Columbus. Her yoga teacher mentioned Caneel Bay to her and she had two weeks of vacation that carried over from last year and she's thirty-three years old and she's a vegetarian. And that's all fine. We interrupt that stream of conversation as I begin to tear away at the edge of my ultrathin condom packet. She gets on top of me. I get on top of her. She stares into my eyes and I stare at the phone, that blinking red light.

"Don't worry about it," Lucy says, hooking her legs around my hips, gently kissing the bruise under my eye. She really has a very beautiful, ugly nose. It makes me want to fuck her that much harder. It's like a sneer. A taunt. I can't stop looking at it. It's the only real imperfection, I realize, in this whole perfect, silent resort.

Afterward, I listen to the wet slap of Lucy's feet on the white, octagonal tiles as she heads to the bathroom. I wonder why they have to be so squeaky clean and white, as if we were in some kind of tourist morgue, our memories wiped away as soon as we departed, the next batch ushered in. I don't want to admit there is something distinctly depressing about a paradise that does not need you.

I stare at the slowly moving fan, some kind of stained wood and wicker number, with frosted glass bulbs jiggling below. Picking up the receiver, I dial for my messages. They're all from Lee, and she sounds agitated. She says she's been trying to reach me since yesterday. Dr. Tolson wants me to call him immediately.

"What's wrong?" Lucy says, standing naked at the foot of the bed. "Is it the scar?"

"No," I say, staring at the raised ridge of flesh on her stomach. "Just got distracted. Tell me more about growing up in Columbus. Did you want to kill yourself?"

"It's Dayton, silly," she says, climbing into bed again. "And yes, I did try to kill myself."

"Oh," I say softly as she nuzzles my neck.

I turn off the light, finding myself wishing I were lying next to Barb. Allowing myself to miss her and Jack for the first time. Allowing myself exactly one minute. I'm staring at the red number on the digital alarm clock.

12:42.

12:43.

"What are you thinking about?" Lucy says.

"Nothing," I say, turning my face toward her. "I was just zoning out."

I buff her skin with my hand, moving over her breasts, that scar, and the racing stripe of dark pubic hair.

"Isn't this the greatest place in the world?" she says.

I wake up, blinking at searing bars of sunlight and white furniture. It takes me five seconds to realize where I am, and when it sinks in, I find that I'm disappointed it's not snowing outside.

"What's wrong with you?" I ask myself, grabbing the phone. I retrieve yesterday's message from Lee and write down Dr. Tolson's phone number. His secretary puts me on hold and I wander to the balcony with the portable.

"Paul," Dr. Tolson says. "I've been trying to reach you."

"I'm on vacation," I say, sitting by the slightly rusted table, the soles of my feet warmed by red tiles.

"Listen," he says. "I have some bad news."

"I'm in St. John," I say. "Have you ever been to St. John?"

Nonsensically, I think that by asking him this, we can start the whole conversation over.

"Once. Long ago. Lovely place. Listen, the chest X-ray came back."

"It's another perfect day," I say. "I mean, it's almost intimidating. Have you ever been parasailing?"

"Paul," Dr. Tolson says.

He's determined, for some odd reason, to tell me that I have cancer. After all that faking, it's really spread. But I'm not going to let that happen. I hang up the phone. I unplug the phone cord. I unplug the jack from the wall and, gripping it in my fist, throw it as far as I can. It hits a palm frond and lands on the well-groomed lawn, where it is immediately spotted by one of the uniformed groundskeepers. He rushes to it as though I had tossed an infant over the balcony, picking it up and looking at me with a hurt expression on his face.

"I don't want to be bothered," I yell at him.

Serious cancer can really ruin your day. *If* you let it.

I choose to rise above it. After all, Dr. Tolson never got to tell me what he saw on the chest X-ray. As far as I'm concerned, it might have been anything. It might have been some funny shape, like I can see in those clouds on the horizon. There—a rhinoceros. No, an alligator. And what does an X-ray come down to anyway but a doctor looking at clouds? The clouds of my fucking lungs.

A red and blue and green fish is swimming around my leg. Its lips barely touching my calf before it circles again.

"What?" I shout down at the water.

The fish declines to respond. Instead, it circles my leg again, dives down and kisses my foot. I step back, but this fish has it in for me. It tastes something on my skin. How much of the fucking world is water and the one cancer-sniffing fish in the universe has to find me?

Or maybe it's all fate. Maybe I never had a chance.

I back out of the water, chased by that flapping fish all the way to the white sand. I sit down and put my head in my hands until one of the groundskeepers comes sweeping.

And how silly it seems now, especially now. That somewhere, someone thought it would be a great idea to employ a man to sweep sand. Of all the useless ideas in the world.

But that's something only I would appreciate. And every other asshole who has serious cancer.

"Sir," the sandsweeper says. "Are you all right? Do you want a hat?"

"Sure," I say, just so he'll go away. I just feel immensely tired suddenly. As if I hadn't slept for a week. I can't conceive of the energy it'll take just to stand up and look like I'm on vacation. Alex, wherever she is in the great blue beyond, is laughing her ass off. And Jack, that little shit, must have known all along. He must have smelled it, just like that fish.

"I'll come visit," I say to him in my mind again, watching him fade away on that people mover at the airport.

"I know you will."

# CHAPTER 11

I'M THE ONLY patient in Dr. Tolson's waiting room who has a killer tan. A rich, creamy, organic kind of tan that extends all the way to my clenched fingers. Never mind that it's thirty-nine degrees on a decrepit, gray New York City day. Never mind that I'm about to have the most depressing doctor's appointment of my entire life. I look like I'm between vacations.

When the nurse calls my name, a few patients in the waiting room briefly look up from their magazines. Despite my tan, they know I'm still one of them, walking sheepishly behind the nurse as she leads me through the door to the examining rooms, one hand pressed firmly in the small of my back, as if, at any point, I might need immediate consolation.

I'm shown into an examining room about halfway down the corridor, right next to my usual room. It isn't until I'm left alone that I realize it's the one in which Alex got her bad news.

Alone in the white room, I unbutton my shirt and sit half-naked and slack-shouldered on the edge of the table. Drawing back the baby blue curtain, I frown at myself in the mirror, dust some peeling skin off my shoulders. There's nothing like the sight of a body that has no idea what it's in for. I look perfectly healthy. Maybe a little soft around the middle, a few unnecessary hairs sprouting here and there, but not like somebody who's on the verge of turning into biological sludge. A cellular compost heap. Everything, in fact, seems more normal than ever. The nurses are having a conversation in the corridor about their Thanksgiving plans. The sounds of traffic come from outside the drawn blind.

I'm thinking of Alex standing naked on that balcony, just over a month ago. I'm thinking of her sitting on the edge of this examining table, looking into this very same mirror. How it all must have seemed just as farfetched to her. Almost ridiculous.

There's a knock at the door, and the handle immediately turns. Why knock at all? Bursting into the room, as usual, Dr. Tolson grips my hand, then squeezes my shoulder. When I'm sitting down, we're just about the same height.

"You look great," he says, gravely.

"Thanks," I say, realizing that he wants to get right down to business.

"You're going to be fine," he says. "We're going to get you through this."

"That's what you said to Alex Hivinshki," I say, terrified.

"Who?"

"She was a patient of yours. She died."

"Oh yes," Dr. Tolson says. "Alex."

He seems offended that I've brought up her name. There's no time for history here. There are other patients, in other rooms, anxiously waiting. This is what Dr. Tolson wants me to know he's thinking.

I turn my head slightly, so I can read the first few lines of the pathology report. But Dr. Tolson slaps the folder closed and begins to speak to me.

"Cancer cells from the tumor in your arm . . . "

"The one you cut out."

"Right. Cancer cells . . . "

"Couldn't possibly have spread. Because you cut the tumor out."

"Paul," Dr. Tolson says, laying his hand on my shoulder again.

"There's nothing wrong with me, Dr. Tolson," I say. "I feel terrific."

"It's in both lungs. We're going to have to talk about palliative care."

I'm standing up now, buttoning my dress shirt. As far as I'm concerned it all comes down to location. And clearly, I'm standing in a very bad location. A doctor's office where they give people bad news. But if I simply remove myself from this location, as fast as humanly possible, everything will be all right.

My dress shirt is one button off, all the way down the line. No time to fix that now. I shake Dr. Tolson's hand as I open the door, tuck in my shirttails as I march down the corridor.

"Do you want to schedule a follow-up appointment?" the nurse calls to me as I walk by.

"No," I say with a quick salute. "I'm good."

I guess some of you, moral snobs that you are, might be licking the fat off your fur right about now. The meal you've made of me! And how many of you have been waiting for me to get my just deserts for lying to Lee, for leaving Barb and Jack in the hotel room, waiting for your revenge as I walked like Jesus in my long flowing white robe on that BreathWalk.

I can see your eyes everywhere today. In the plate glass of that Starbucks window. Staring at me from that van. Swerving over Manhattan in your superior little helicopter. Just once you'd think you might have the guts to tell me what you think of me. But no, you still lurk.

I get off at the Seventh Avenue stop in Park Slope.

Peer in the window of the cheese shop, all decked out for Thanksgiving. A hundred unnecessary delicacies crammed into the window. Gumdrops and sculpted fig bars and nuggets of crystallized ginger. The rush-hour line already forming at the counter.

And for some reason, it hits me then. It hits me as I'm staring in that cheese shop window. I'm not going to be around in five years. Maybe three. And who knows, I might be dead in one.

Yet I'm staring at a tin of crystallized ginger, and I can hear the happy sounds of people making ridiculously unimportant decisions at the cheese counter.

Are there any firm guarantees I'll be around next Thanksgiving?

Will anyone miss me?

"Sir," the aproned counterman says, poking his goatee outside the shop door. "Can you please remove your forehead from our window?"

I lift my head and he takes the edge of his striped blue apron and buffs the skin smudge I've left on the glass. This seems to amuse the customers crammed in the store, who seem to be relishing the stricken, idiotic expression on my face. That is, until I keep on looking at them, rooted to the spot. One by one, they turn away, fidgeting with the clasps of wallets or handbags or checking their cell phones. And I turn away, too, walking a few blocks until I enter a used bookstore.

"Can I help you?" an older, frumpy woman says, her green sweater dotted with stray balls of cotton.

"No," I say, "I'm fine."

I browse the nonfiction pile by the window, but can't find anything sufficiently depressing. At a time like this, I need someone truly evil to distract me.

I need Hitler.

But this is a difficult person to ask for in a tiny bookstore in Park Slope, where a large Hasidic woman is reading to her four expressionless sons in the children's section.

There he is, on the next-to-top shelf. I reach up and *Last Mystery of the Third Reich* nearly topples on me. I right it just in time, and look over to make sure the Hasidic woman isn't watching. I look in the other direction, too, and I'm surprised to see Brenda's husband, Felipe, standing there. Just standing there, back to the window, hands in the pockets of his Ralph Lauren jacket, shifting from one leg to another. It seems like forever since Brenda and I flirted over that blackened tilapia, and I wonder if she might have told him about her affair with me. For a moment, I think he might even be following me. But if he were following me, he wouldn't just be standing in front of a bookstore. And when he turns toward the window, it's not me he's looking at, it's his reflection. He runs two fingers through his curly hair and gives himself a quick once-over, so focused on his own appearance, he misses me completely.

Definitely waiting for someone. Maybe some hot blind date.

I'm watching his back through the window when a woman swoops in out of nowhere and, grinning, plants a kiss on his cheek. They hug briefly, and then he grabs her hand and they walk away.

My wife, I mean. Lee. He walks away with Lee.

I'm stunned. All I can do is look down at the book. At Hitler sitting on the terrace of the Berghof, one hand scratching the head of his favorite German shepherd, Blondie. And stunned by what I've seen, all I can do is read the caption over and over again, somewhat comforted by the fact that by the end of the war the Führer felt that even his beloved dog was plotting against him.

"I'm sorry," Lee says again.

I've lost count, to tell you the truth. That might be the thirteenth apology, or the thirtieth. I just sit here on the couch and let them float down on me, like so much dandruff on my shoulders, and even more useless.

"But I'm dying," I say softly. "Didn't that make you think twice?"

"It did," she says, perching on the sofa chair, making a triangle with her hands. "But you made it impossible for me to be close to you."

"Bullshit," I say. "You just want to have kids. You're just moving on. Why not steal poor Brenda's husband."

"Poor Brenda?" Lee says, giving me a knowing look.

And that's it, I tell myself. Five years of marriage. Done.

Not that fast, of course. We talk until three in the morning. It all could have been said in three minutes. But we go over everything again and again, like faithful accountants making sure they haven't missed a very important deduction. We haven't missed anything. I've been in it for her mother's money, and she's been in it for the kids. And all I can say is, go home to your loved ones tonight, and clue them in. Tell them you're not who they thought you were. Tell them you run around with shit-stained underwear on your head when they leave for work. Tell them you enjoy reading about constipated toddlers. Tell them you fart on crowded subway cars and savor the pinched faces of your fellow commuters.

Tell them you're an alcoholic, an insomniac, have an orgasm inferiority complex, smile idiotically at kittens dancing on shredded paper in a pet shop window, blew off your best friend in Europe before he committed suicide, slept with your brother.

Because I know you, and I sense it all the way from here. It's all starting to fall apart.

Or maybe that's just me.

Of course, I'd underestimated my wife. I'd underestimated everyone. And my father had warned me against doing just this. The man of 573 women, on his hospital deathbed, had squeezed my elbow so tightly I winced. And then, in a very loving voice, he warned me not to ever marry someone smarter than me.

"That's how," he whispered, rubbing together his dry fingers like kindling, "you get away with things."

But who, really, in the entire history of mankind, has ever gotten away with anything? My mother found my father's little brown book. Dr. Tolson found cancer in my lungs. And Hitler's own dog betrayed him.

It's my turn to say I'm sorry. It's my turn to tell Lee I slept with Brenda. It's my turn to tell her I never had cancer. But I have it now, I really do. And I'm terrified. So terrified that I shouldn't care how many times she's already had sex with Felipe. Useless details! I've got real perspective now.

"How many times did you fuck him?" I shout at her.

"You," she says, practically gleaming with pleasure, "are really something. I feel sorry for you."

She shakes her head very knowingly and very slowly.

"That's a nice thing to say to a dying man," I say.

But actually, when I think about it, it is about the only thing you can say to a dying man.

# CHAPTER 12

"TO TELL YOU the truth," Terry says, passing me a plate heaped with stringy sweet potatoes, "I never really liked her."

"Terry," Eric barks, "they're not even divorced."

I've been invited to Thanskgiving dinner by Eric. At first, I laughed at the thought of it. But after spending a week alone in my apartment, leaving increasingly desperate messages on my mother-in-law's voice mail, whose mansion in Connecticut Lee had escaped to, I found myself grateful to be in New Jersey. It felt like some kind of unavoidable surrender. I eased the Mazda into the small driveway, and turned off the ignition, and quietly thought: This would be a fine place to end it all. Looking at this rotten fence through the entrails of that bare brush. They could bury me right there, under that grill my brother's not allowed to use.

Instead, I pass the sweet potatoes. I listen to Eric

mildly defend my wife. Fortunately, it's all the conversation we're capable of having, because the baby is bucking around in the Exersaucer, throwing up his hands.

"What do you want?" Terry says, wagging her head at the baby.

"Booby," says the three-year-old brother, crushing some peas with the back of his spoon.

"You want some booby?" Terry asks the baby.

"Jesus," Eric says. "Some class?"

"Get over yourself," Terry says, leaping up from the table with such energy that even the baby looks concerned. Now Terry's raising her arms and the baby isn't. He blinks at her once and pukes something green down his shirt. Then he smiles.

"Cigarette?" Eric says to me.


"What happened out here?" I say, staring at the burned bits of grass and torched floorboards we're standing on.

"Oh nothing," Eric says, lighting my cigarette. "Leaves caught fire. Couldn't remember where the hell the fire extinguisher was though. Has that ever happened to you?"

I take a drag and look more closely at the destruction on the porch. The fire had eaten through a third of it before he managed to put it out. And I had seen it all, in that vision I had back in Minneapolis. Alone on that icy field. For some reason, this makes me intensely happy. For

the first time since I left Minneapolis, I have that delight-
ful sense of uncertainty again. There's someone behind all
this scenery, I know it. There's a reason things happen.

"I saw it," I tell Eric.

"Saw what?" he says, taking extra care to ash his cigarette in a clay pot pre-approved for the purpose. Even
the pile of dead leaves has been dutifully cleaned up.

"This house burning."

"The house didn't *burn*," he says. "Goddamn it. Why
does everyone have to make such a big deal about this?"

I decide to say nothing more. Better to leave it in
that dreamy crawlspace, where we still have revelations
and save ourselves. Back here, it's a cold Thanksgiving,
and we're just back to chipping away at something.

"Terry wants to have another kid."

"Are you serious?" I say.

"Yeah," he says, shaking his head as if he has no
choice in the matter.

"Well," I say. "Good for you."

"What?" he says, looking at me incredulously.

"You're alive," I nearly scream at him. "You're
spawning. This is good."

"I can't tell if you're joking."

"Only half."

"What happened to you out there?" he says.

"Nothing," I say, as Jack's face bursts into my mind.
Getting smaller and smaller on that people mover.

Crouching down, one after the other, we mash out our cigarettes in the clay pot and cringe as Terry shouts through the screen door.

"The pie," she yells at Eric. "Defrost it."

The funny thing about really getting serious cancer is that I had to go *back* to work. I had to do *something*. I couldn't sit on the couch all day toggling between the thought of what might be happening inside my lungs and the thought of Lee sleeping with Felipe. Besides, just to numb myself, I'd swallowed the last of the pain medication in the back of the medicine cabinet. Old pill bottles we'd never thrown away filled with a few stray Vicodin and Tylenol with codeine. I crushed up the pills and diced them all together, and then I snorted lines on a wedding photograph of me and Lee. I didn't have the heart to pull an Alex, but I could erase myself slowly.

The Monday after Thanksgiving I found myself back on the PATH train, aluminum coffee thermos dangling from my hand. I found myself back at my old desk, rearranging the mess some freelancer had made. I was informed by Greg Boyden that Lisa Hunt had been covering for me, and, he added, she'd been doing a pretty good job. But would I mind explaining DFOG to her once and for all?

Sure, I said.

And this is why, late Monday afternoon, already pitch-black outside, I'm staring at my old screensaver. That barn in the middle of nowhere. The bleary twilight still leaking through that web of twigs. I can smell the double espresso hot chocolate before I even see Lisa Hunt. She sets the cup down on my desk, goes back to get her chair, and then squeezes in next to me. Her black bangs have been straightened and she even looks like she's lost a little weight. Under the fluorescent strips, her lipstick gleams. She takes a sip of coffee and her gaping brown eyes size me up. Maybe it's all the Vicodin I snorted over the last forty-eight hours, the hazy expression on my face, the distinct lack of posture. Maybe it's the half-shaved hairs on my neck. But Lisa Hunt smiles and rolls the boulder of her kneecap up against my calf until I wince in pain. She knows I'm defenseless.

"Hurts," I say softly.

"Where were we?" she says, ignoring me.

"DFOG."

"Take a sip of my delicious coffee," she orders me. "You look a little sleepy."

Obediently, I take a sip of coffee and begin to explain DFOG, aware that Lisa's gleaming lips are coming closer to my ear. The humidity of her breath crawling down my eustachian tube.

"I knew you'd come back," she says, pulling the

front of my chair seat toward her and giving me one quick, wet kiss on the cheek.

I make a few unnecessary keystrokes, but on the whole I take it pretty well. My self esteem is at such low tide that I don't even bother to wipe the chilly wetness off my skin.

Monday Night Football. The Rams versus the Panthers. Irrelevant game for an irrelevant life. I sit in the dark as the television sheds its light on my shoes. I have the portable phone in my hand. Barb's telephone number on that piece of paper. Pieces of wet tissue paper dot the rug. I dab my eyes and rip off another square.

"Hang in there," I tell myself. "I'm with you."

You know it's bad when you have to split yourself in two. Or maybe that's a natural reaction when you find out you're going to die. You literally wish you were someone else. *I* do, I mean. You're still out there, healthy, pink-cheeked, flossing your gums in some happy mirror.

But the more I talk to myself, the worse I feel. By halftime, the room is filled with these other selves, other voices, each one a failed friend, just trying to do his best. What on earth could they say to make me feel any better?

I dial Barb's number. On the fourth ring, she picks up.

"Who is this?" she says.

"Paul Mauro," I say, sniffling.

"Paul?" she says, sounding genuinely surprised to hear from me, which is great, because I thought there was a good chance she'd just hang up. "You have a cold or something?"

"No," I say. "Just a little under the weather. How's Jack?"

Silence on the other end. I can almost hear her deciding whether she'll let me get this personal.

"He's doing better."

"What happened?"

"I can't go into that right now. I'm exhausted."

"Anyway," I say, realizing this will be the last time we'll ever speak to each other, "I wanted to say Merry Christmas."

"It's two weeks away," she says. "Are you sure you're okay?"

"I'm fine," I say. "Can I ask you a question?"

"What?" she says sleepily.

"What kind of tree are you getting this year?"

"The same tree we get every year. The fake one that's down in the basement."

And then it hits me. I'm going to be the fucking Cancer Grinch this year. I'm going to come sailing down that cold slope with the biggest fucking Christmas tree Jack's ever seen. The thought of this excites me so much I'm actually standing up, but my pain-killer-laden blood falls immediately to my feet. I pitch forward and my elbow snaps the armrest of Lee's favorite chair.

"Paul?"

"Still here," I say, righting myself. "Listen, I'm coming to visit you."

"Sure," she says sarcastically. "That sounds like a great plan. We can have another one-night stand and you can ditch us in the morning."

"Please," I say. "Give me your address."

Turning on the lamp on the small desk, I flick the cap off a pen with my thumbnail. I find a notepad. There's just silence on the other end. I worry that she's hung up.

"Barb? Are you there?"

"We live in Coventry. It's south of Providence."

"I love Rhode Island."

And right now, at 12:30, on a windy night in Brooklyn, alone in my two-bedroom apartment, I do honestly love Rhode Island. I can already picture myself in the Mazda on I-95, a Styrofoam container of Dunkin Donuts coffee steaming in the cup holder, the radio blasting bad Connecticut music. Bad Company. *I was meant for loving you. You were meant for loving me.*

"Why don't you just send us a nice card?" she says. I can tell that she's warming up to the idea. And the sound of her warming up to it makes me feel terrific.

"I'm bringing you a Christmas tree," I tell her. "I'm going to hog-tie it to the roof of my car."

"Sure," she says.

But she asks me if I have a pen. I write her address sideways. Long blue lines. A scrawl that all my other selves huddle around and try to read.

At dawn on Tuesday, one week before Christmas, I'm staked out on Fourth Avenue in Sunset Park in the Mazda, waiting for two Mexican guys in hooded sweatshirts to finish unloading a truckload of stunted pine trees. I haven't slept all night. Maybe the dark circles under my eyes alarm them, or the cigarettes I've been chain-smoking and tossing out the window, but one of the workers pulls down the bill of his yellow Yankees cap and raps his knuckles on my passenger window. I unroll it with a polite smile on my face, my nostril-spewed nicotine interlacing with his frozen breath.

"You a cop?"

"No," I say. "I just want to buy a tree."

"We don't open till eight, Mister. We've got to unload the truck."

"That's okay," I say. "Take your time."

He walks away, shaking his head.

"Loco," he says to his coworker, twirling a finger around his ear. "Traeme un arbol."

The other guy smirks, pulls up the rear door of the truck, and begins tossing out Christmas trees.

But my manic, good mood must be infectious because a few minutes later, the same guy comes back with an eight-foot spruce in his hand. I roll the window down again.

"Thirty bucks," he says.

I get out of the car, touch the nettles, eye its underparts. I try to picture it inside a cozy living room somewhere in the boondocks of Rhode Island. I try to picture Jack being impressed.

"Bigger," I say.

A few minutes later, the other worker tosses another pine prisoner out of the truck. They give me the works, running it through a tree-shaker and netting-baler, and they even tie it to the roof of my car. I give them forty bucks and thank them too many times. By eight o'clock I'm on the interstate, constantly checking my rearview mirror to make sure that all the pine needles haven't already blown off.

By the time I pull into the rest stop in North Haven, I'm exhausted. I sit inside the McDonald's, slowly eating French fries, eyeing the tree on top of my Mazda with suspicion, as if I had no idea how it had gotten there. All the best ideas seem idiotic at a distance. So I crumple up the paper bag, toss it in the wastebin, and head back to the car before I can change my mind.

# CHAPTER 13

SIPPING AT MY gigantic cup of coffee, keeping one eye on the crumpled Mapquest page, I manage to get to Coventry in under four hours. The cloudless sky is tinged with pink by the time I pull right onto Hollyhock Lane, casing the split-level homes and their identical asphalt driveways until I come to 271. It's another split-level, with a wide brick chimney and a well-kept yard. There's one other noticeable detail: a flagpole planted right in the middle of the lawn. And at the top, forty feet up, an enormous American flag, snapping in the wind. There's even a faded blue BUSH/CHENEY sign in the bay window.

"You're kidding," I say softly. So Barb's some kind of right-wing patriot. My Christmas fantasy is already coming off the rails. If I don't turn around now, I'll be spending it with a bunch of strangers wearing tight red sweaters, bowing their heads at the dining room table and linking hands in prayer.

"Paul," Barb says, cracking the screen door. She's wearing a red T-shirt that says BATTLING BADGERS and a pair of faded jeans. As she walks up to the car, she hugs herself against the cold and dances across the cold grass. I smile as I roll the window down, feeling as if I've known her for years. She leans in and gives me a kiss on the cheek, rubs her hands together. It's only then that I notice how puffy her eyes are. And bloodshot, too. I wonder if she hasn't slept, or if she's been crying.

"Nice tree," she says.

I get out of the car, nod my head at the tree, which has kept most of its pine needles.

"Nice flag," I say, as I follow her to the house.

"My ex," Barb says, not even bothering to look up. "He put it up when the war started. I haven't had the time to get it removed."

"Or the sign," I say.

"The sign, too," she says, giving me a funny look. "Don't worry, I'm not a Republican."

I want to tell her how relieved I am, but figure that would make me sound as if I were halfhearted about her in the first place. Instead, I follow her inside the house. The small kitchen reeks of burned coffee. The stereo in the other room is turned up high, blasting out some pop song.

Barb excuses herself and turns the music down. I stand in front of the coffee-maker watching a black drop fizzle on the hot plate. And then another. I turn the machine off. The carafe sits on the kitchen table, next to an empty yellow mug. Strewn over the whole table, like blueprints, are Jack's hospital papers. Bills. Insurance breakdowns. Blood tests. Doctors' names. A WebMD printout about a bone marrow–suspension drug. The coffee mug has made its mark everywhere, leaving its crusty semicircle all over the information.

"I'm just trying to stay awake," Barb says, walking back into the kitchen. Leaning against the dishwasher, she purses her lips and stares sideways.

"Jack's not doing well?"

"No," she says. "He's not. He's bleeding inside. They switched him to Clolar."

"I'm sorry," I say.

I stand up and walk toward her. She's still looking sideways. And when I embrace her, she's so tense she doesn't even turn to face me. In fact, she's so preoccupied it takes a moment for my embrace to sink in. And when it does, she wrestles herself away.

"So did you come all this way to get laid?"

"Of course not," I lie.

"How's your wife?"

"We're getting a divorce."

"Listen," she says, forcing a tired smile. "This isn't going to work. It's my fault. I should have told you not to come."

"All right," I say. "I understand. I'll just get the tree. How about we just decorate the tree? It'll be a nice surprise for Jack. And then I'll just drive away. You won't see me again. Fair enough?"

I walk out the door before she can say no, back under that enormous flag and its lengthening shadow. Reaching into my pocket, I take out my car keys and start to saw at the twine binding the tree. I pull the tree off the roof of my car and balance it on my shoulder, aware that I'm leaving a path of needles. By the time I squeeze it through the kitchen door, it's not a tree anymore, it's a sappy stick, the needles lying everywhere.

"Well, shit," I say, standing the poor thing up.

"Oh," Barb says, covering her mouth in sympathy or amusement, I can't tell which. "But you made the effort."

"It was going to be great," I say, leaning the tree in the corner, by the door.

"It doesn't matter anyway," Barb says. "Jack's doctor says there's a good chance he'll still be in the hospital for Christmas."

Telling me this brings her to the verge of tears.

"Paul?" she says.

"Yeah?"

"I have to trust you. Because I can't even think straight."

The phone starts to ring, just as I'm about to

reassure Barb that I'm not going to sneak out at dawn again. But she doesn't even seem to notice the sound.

"Your phone is ringing," I say.

"That's Tony, my ex," she says. "He calls me twenty times a day. I don't even answer it anymore."

"You should call the police," I say. "That's harassment."

"I will," she says. "When I get the time. I've got more important things to think about right now."

The phone finally stops ringing. I'm just about to ask her if I should leave when it starts ringing again.

"Hey," she says, grabbing my hand. "You want to go for a ride?"

There's something about being driven around by Barb in a big, flame-red Dodge Durango that makes me feel a little emasculated. Everyone seems to know her here in Coventry. She makes a right at a red light and people wave. We drive through the parking lot of the bank and people wave. We get gas and people wave. Everywhere, people seem to do double takes when they see the SUV, and their arms jump up almost automatically, and they wave.

"You're popular here," I say, wondering what all of these people must make of me, the guy they've never seen before.

"It's Jack," she says wearily. "Everybody knows about it. He's like the town mascot now."

She takes me on a tour of town, wryly describing all the main attractions.

"That's Johnson's Pond," she says, pulling over to the shoulder of the road so I can get a better look at the cold blue pond, some seagulls scattering themselves on the surface and reassembling again.

"Very pretty," I say.

"Jack and I skate there when it freezes over."

For a moment, I just follow her gaze and picture what I know she's picturing. Jack and her, the blades of their skates catching the sun, his short legs pushing off, trying to catch up to her. I can see him falling, getting up, the delayed ricochet of his voice calling after her.

"Anyway," she says, pulling back onto the road, honking at a passing car as it speeds by.

"Maybe we'll all skate there when he gets out of the hospital."

"Maybe," she says, speeding by the other historical attractions with a word or two of description.

A cannon from the Civil War.

A clapboard Victorian that was once a waystation for escaped slaves.

A Unitarian church with a concrete steeple and a thought of the day posted outside: *Don't be afr id of the fork in the ro d.*

"Don't be afrid of the fork in the rod," I repeat.

"There's always some letters missing," she says,

glancing at the church in her rearview mirror. "When I was in high school we used to rearrange all the letters. We came up with some pretty astonishing thoughts."

Barb pulls into the parking lot of the Wal-Mart and turns off the ignition.

"I'll be right back," she says.

"Where are you going?" I say, a little helplessly. "I thought we were going to visit Jack in the hospital."

"I told him I'd bring him a Nutter Butter," she says, slamming the door.

Nutter Butter, I repeat to myself, watching her walk away, hands jammed into the pockets of her white parka. An older woman pushing a shopping cart waves to her as Barb walks into the store. Barb pretends not to notice. Keeping her chin pinned to her chest, she walks through the automatic doors.

I'm listening to the car radio, eased back in the seat. I'm wondering if I could live here, playfully tossing the concept around my mind, when I hear a sharp knock on the passenger window.

Broad-shouldered guy. Wearing a red microfleece jacket and a pair of khakis. Almost bald, except for a peninsula of well-clipped brown hair that seems to point directly between his small, unkind blue eyes to the rest of his unshaven face. This must be Barb's ex, and I can instantly see why a woman might want to get away from him. But what does he want with me?

"How's it going?" I say, through six inches of open window. This mode of communication doesn't seem to be adequate for him, so he walks around the car, opens the door, and climbs into the driver's seat.

"How do you like it?" he says, staring at me.

"Great ride," I say, trying to smile, until it dawns on me all at once that humor is *not* going to save the day.

"Are you comfortable?" he says. "You look a little cramped."

I toggle the button on the side of the seat and glide backward while smiling at him. Great view of the stubble under his chin. Two tiny whiteheads on his neck he probably has no idea even exist.

"I'm Paul," I say, stretching out my hand. It must look like I'm asking him to help me up.

"I'm Tony," he says, gripping my hand very tightly. "Get out of my fucking car."

"No problem," I say, opening the door and doing exactly as I'm told. But apparently, the fact that I'm standing outside his car isn't going to be enough to satisfy him, because he's walking around the hood again.

"Hold on," he says, almost politely, and I do, smiling at him as if we were going to shake hands again, but when he gets close enough, he swings his right leg back and kicks my ass. Literally.

I lurch forward and grab my burning buttock with one hand. I can still feel the exact shape of his loafer in my glute.

There's something undeniably humiliating about being a grown man and getting kicked in the ass in a public space. Even an old lady pushing a shopping cart filled with Depends stops and looks horrified.

"Was that really necessary?" I say, keeping my eyes on him and bumping into an empty shopping cart. It spins toward Tony and he violently pushes it away and takes another step toward me.

"Okay," I say, holding up my hands. "I'll walk."

This seems to work, because he turns his head slightly to the right, as if he were distracted by something more important. And then he suddenly flinches, as if I were about to throw a punch.

Tony deflects the pack of Nutter Butters with his elbow and steps back.

"Get back in my car, Paul," Barb says. But I'm frozen. I'm watching Tony stoop down and pick up the pack of Nutter Butters. There's a smirk on his face as he tosses them back to Barb.

"What a great mother you are," Tony says. "Buying that crap for Jack. Driving around with this dipshit so everyone can see."

These two don't waste any time, I'm thinking, watching Barb walk toward him. Their face-off is ruined by the sound of a car horn, tapped twice. About twenty feet away, a redhead with clumps of mascara on her eyelashes sits in a silver BMW waiting. Raising her long fingernails like claws, she taps the heel of her hand on the steering wheel and toots the horn again.

"There Tony," Barb says sarcastically, waving to the woman inside the BMW. "Your getaway car is here."

"Nice to meet you, Paul," Tony says to me, winking once before climbing into the car, which speeds away before he's even closed the door.

"Are you coming with me?" Barb says, looking at me over her shoulder.

# CHAPTER 14

HOSPITALS ARE LIKE airports. Once you've seen one you've seen them all. The Elaine Butler Medical Center is just a little seedier, a little smaller. The gleaming linoleum tiles buckling in places. A piece of dry chewing gum stuck on an oil painting of one of the benefactors. A vending machine out of order. Just a hint here and there that you might not be getting the best care in the world. Barb hasn't said a word since we left the car. And when the elevator opens on the third floor, she races ahead. It's not the first time today it's crossed my mind that I should just leave. But I follow her down the hallway, which is painted with happy orange and yellow stripes, and into Jack's room. As I watch her pull back the curtain, I'm aware of the slightly acrid smell of vomit.

Jack's asleep, the white silk hem of a cotton blanket pulled up to his chin, but his arm hangs out. There's an IV taped to his wrist, the skin smudged with orange

Betadine, and he looks much too thin. I start to whisper something to Barb and it wakens Jack. He blinks at his mother, then at me.

"Did you bring the Nutter Butters?" he asks her.

"Right here," she says, placing them on his bedside table.

"I feel like I'm going to throw up again," he says, looking at his wrist.

"I thought they weren't going to start you before noon," Barb says, looking at the IV bag labeled CLOLAR hanging above his head.

Barb kisses him on the forehead, then sits down in the chair next the bed. She holds Jack's hand while he stares up at the football game on the TV. The volume's been turned down.

"Demetrius is playing today," he says. "I wish we were back in Minnesota."

She looks up at me and shrugs her shoulders.

"Paul came a long way to see you," she says. "Remember, last night I told you he was coming."

"I don't feel like talking to him."

"That's not nice, Jack. He brought a tree with him."

"We already have a tree."

"I think he wants to say hello, Jack."

I'm looking at the stuffed animals lined up on the windowsill, a foil balloon kissing the plate-glass window. The crop of greeting cards propped up on the bedside table and all those good, heartfelt wishes, written at a slant. Jack doesn't need more attention or love. He's maxed out. The whole town's sponsoring him now. Keeping him in their thoughts. Praying for him.

"What's that?" I ask Barb, pointing to an enormous wooden key on the window ledge.

"Oh," she says. "The mayor stopped by. Gave him the key to the town."

"It doesn't open anything," Jack says glumly. "It's fake."

"I'll let you two catch up," Barb says, walking into the bathroom, closing the door.

"You're not supposed to use that one, Mom," Jack shouts, his face still turned away from me. "It's only for patients."

His raised voice immediately brings a nurse into the room.

"Jack?" she says.

"Hi Laura," Jack says, turning his head. "My wrist hurts."

"Just a few more hours to go, okay sweetheart?" she says, touching the catheter in his wrist.

Jack screams out in pain. Barb comes bursting out of the bathroom, fly still open, thumb hooked around the top button of her pants, her black panties just visible at the hip. And in this confusing moment, a voice in my head is asking me a question.

Is she wearing those black panties for me? Or does she wear them all the time?

"I heard you scream," she says, buttoning her jeans. "What the hell is going on?"

"Everything's fine," the nurse says, reddening. "I'll leave you all alone."

"Jack," Barb says, sitting back down in the chair and cocking her head. "Were you really in that much pain?"

"Yes," Jack says angrily. "And can you zip up your pants please? Paul's checking you out."

You little shit, I'm thinking, affectionately of course. Barb looks at me accusingly, as if she can read my mind.

"You're a real trooper," I say to Jack, nodding my head solemnly.

While Barb watches Jack sleep, I sit outside the emergency room, waiting for an ambulance to come rolling in. Since I found out I have real cancer, my patience with the pace of daily disasters has run out. I want to see car crashes, broken noses, planes falling out of the sky. I want the world to fall apart before I do.

But the world seems to have become even more safe. No emergencies in Coventry today. Only leaves sweeping themselves across the hospital parking lot, the sunset draining out. And when the ambulance finally arrives, it's just some old lady being wheeled out, babbling to the paramedics about a pain in her chest. They've obviously trucked her in before, because neither is listening.

And suddenly it occurs to me, that's why I'm here, besides wanting to get into Barb's pants. Because Jack has it worse than me. I want to hang around the one person I know who can make me feel a little bit better about my own bad situation. At least I'll make it to forty. He'll be lucky if he makes it to nine. Isn't that the truth, I ask myself? Isn't that why I strapped that tree to the roof of the Mazda and drove three hundred miles? And if it isn't, what is my business here?

When I get back to Jack's room, Barb and Jack are both asleep. His wrinkled chemo bag is empty, but the catheter remains taped to his wrist. I sit down in the free chair and watch them. That's when you can really tell who people are, when they're fast asleep. Jack's just a cute, frightened kid, his eyebrows occasionally knotted by some problem in a dream, which is quickly solved because his face relaxes again. But the problem seems to be passed on through the air to Barb, who suddenly lifts her chin, still asleep, and sighs. I watch her head fall again. She hasn't even bothered to put makeup on.

"Everybody all right?" the nurse says, looking in the door, giving me a kind look, as if I were some kind of caretaker, the guy who guards others while they sleep.

"I think so," I say. The doubt in my voice is enough to wipe the smile off her face, and I'm happy about that, because no one should be smiling. And no one should be handing out enormous fake wooden keys to the town either, while we're at it. After the nurse leaves I walk over to the window and pick up the key, painted a greenish gold color. I turn it in the air, imagining that I am unlocking some impossibly heavy door, my eyes widening at a heap of precious metal, as if that would make any difference in the world now. I put the key back on the window ledge and lean against the wall, squeezing my eyelids shut. I've closed my tired eyes for about five seconds when I hear the sound of voices in the hallway.

Standing up, I rub my face and listen to a discussion taking place just outside the room.

"Is this the room?"

My heart sinks as five well-wishers file into the room. Two older men, one short and white-haired, the other taller and balding. Followed in by two middle-aged ladies, one brunette and one blond, both wearing lots of greasy blue eyeshadow. Last in the room is a gangly kid wearing a Patriots cap that he takes off as soon as he sees Jack, as if this were somehow respectful. Barb instantly wakes up when she hears them shuffling in, her mouth tightening as she watches them. This doesn't make any sense to me. It's like five people just walked into the wrong hospital room, but they're all filing past Jack as he sleeps. The aging blonde quickly crosses herself at the foot of Jack's bed.

"You don't have to be so morbid," Barb whispers to her.

"It's okay, Barbara," the tall guy standing next to me says. "Margaret's just saying a little prayer for him."

"She can say it somewhere else," Barb says, staring fiercely at Margaret.

The whispered disagreement wakes Jack up. He squints at everyone surrounding him, then closes his eyes again.

"Hey Jack," says the shorter man with the white hair. He stoops over the bed and gently squeezes Jack's hand. "We brought you something."

Jack twists his lips to one side, but his eyes remain closed.

The tall guy next to me gently places the gift-wrapped package on Jack's covered legs. Jack's eyes flicker open and he stares at the shiny red wrapping.

"What is it?" he says glumly.

"Well, you have to open it, champ," the short guy says.

Before the man even finishes his sentence, Jack's torn through the paper and opened the box inside.

"There's a card," the brunette says, a little disappointed that Jack hasn't even bothered to look at it. "It's from Coach Remson."

Jack holds the orange and green uniform by the sleeves, looking at the word *Bulldogs* stitched across the front, then lays it over his knees, tracing the number 4 on the back.

"Six buttons. Hot off the press," the tall guy next to me says. "Coach sends his best."

"Spring will be here before you know it, Jack," the short guy says. "Better start working on that curveball. Pete'll give you some tips. Right Pete?"

Pete, the gangly teenager standing by the bathroom, looks like the spacey kid who's suddenly been called on in class.

"Sure," Pete says, taking a few steps forward. "Whenever."

"Thanks," Barb says, with a quick, forced smile, taking the uniform from Jack. At a loss for anything else to say, the relatives all watch her carefully fold it and place it by the window, next to the foil balloons and the greeting cards. Then she gathers the torn wrapping paper, crumples it into a wrinkled red ball, and lobs it into the wastebasket, where it lands with a muted thump. It's clear that she's trying to cut the visit short, but our guests have no intention of leaving. They might not have anything else to say, but they're definitely staying put. The blonde who was praying before has even settled down in the chair next to Jack's bed.

"I'll be outside," I say to Barb, hooking a thumb toward the door, but I haven't even taken a step before I run into Tony and his girlfriend. She's wearing large brown sunglasses and carrying an enormous stuffed rabbit in her arms. They both push past me as if I weren't even there. I watch as Tony holds up his hand and Jack weakly smacks his palm. Then the goggle-eyed rabbit is thrust upon him.

This is followed by what seems like a minute of backslapping, kissing, and hugging as Tony makes his way around the room.

"We just brought Jack the new uniform," someone says.

"Oh yeah," Tony says. "Where is it?"

"Barbara put it on the windowsill."

Tony grabs the uniform and shakes it out. He holds it against his blue dress shirt.

"Awesome," he says, turning toward Barb. "Four. Great number. Right, Barb?"

Barb ignores Tony and leans over Jack, giving him a quick kiss good-bye.

"Mom," Jack says. "Where are you going?"

"She's not going anywhere," Tony says, tossing the uniform on the windowsill again. "Right, Mom? The party's just starting."

I follow Barb out of the room, glancing over my shoulder one last time at Jack, whose cheeks have been seized by the redhead. As fast as we're leaving, we still can't escape the sound of her giant, fake kiss.

For a long time, I sit in the Durango with Barb, not saying anything. She's looking up at the window on the third floor, where Jack is still enduring his visitors. It's dark now, so we can easily see the people gathered in his room. They talk to one another, then suddenly look down. I wonder if Jack's fallen asleep again.

"So that's Tony's side of the family?" I say, just to fill the silence.

"Yeah," she says, gripping the steering wheel. "I want to kill them. Just for wasting Jack's time."

"Must be tough dealing with that," I say, putting my hand on her shoulder, but she moves away.

"What do you know?" Barb says, staring at me angrily, her lips thinned out. "For all I know you're even worse than them. I don't even know who you are."

"You're right," I say. "I don't know what it feels like. I'll just shut up."

I'm looking up at Jack's window, watching the television's light flicker on the wall, when I hear Barb groan. She doesn't want me to touch her, and I can't say anything, so all I can do is watch her cry. Tears just roll down the side of her nose, fall off her chin, and stick to her sweater like beads.

"I feel so powerless," she says, sliding two fingers across her eyes, rubbing the wetness on her jeans. "I wake up every morning, and I can't believe this is really happening."

"Listen," I say. "If it's easier for you, I could just take off."

I mean, it would be easier for *me*. But I need her to ask. I owe her that.

"How do you feel when you wake up?" she says, ignoring my question. "Are you scared shitless about dying? How do you deal with it?"

"You've just got to go on," I hear myself say. "One step at a time. It takes a lot of courage."

The great thing about dying is that so many people have done it before, you really don't have to reinvent the wheel. Just haul out the old clichés you've heard a hundred times before.

"Everything becomes sweeter, in a funny kind of way," I say. "I don't really sweat the small stuff anymore."

Barb's giving me a confused look, and then something seems to clear in her mind.

"So it hasn't hit you yet," she says, putting the SUV into reverse.

"What are you talking about?" I say. "Of course it's hit me. I'm dying. I have fucking *cancer*."

"I know you do, Paul," she says softly. "No one's questioning that."

We cruise through Coventry again. I glare at the bank, the gas station, the CVS, wondering how she could possibly insult a dying man. It's not my problem she doesn't have full custody of her kid. Why does she have to take it out on me?

We drive in silence for awhile, that old familiar silence that used to harden between Lee and me. I didn't come this far just to feel the same.

*Maybe you're right,* I should say. *Maybe I'm just full of shit.* But I don't. Instead, I just point at the windshield and the thin crease of blue expiring on the horizon. A fistful of stars already tossed out into the blackness above.

"It's beautiful out here," I say.

"I know," she says sadly.

# CHAPTER 15

I'VE EXAGGERATED SOMEWHAT. The tree I've brought from Brooklyn does have a few intact pine needles attached to its limbs, and when Barb and I get back to the house, she brings the Christmas ornaments up from the basement and we begin to decorate it.

"Shit," she says. "I forgot the crèche. Can you get it for me? It's by the washing machine. Take the flashlight. I haven't had time to change the bulb down there."

I pick up the heavy black flashlight and walk down into the basement. Feel my way down a flight of plywood stairs. When I get to the bottom it sounds like I'm stepping on candy wrappers, but when I train the beam at my feet, I see it's only dead horseflies. It smells like a sigh from the underworld down here. I wave the flashlight and the washer and drier are revealed, then a bunch of shrouded baby toys. There's a three-speed Schwinn with a flat tire. A few scattered tennis rackets. A broken fishing rod. A Steel Force 150 crossbow with cool-looking olive and brown camouflage. I lay the flashlight on the drier and pick up the weapon. I try to draw back the cord, but I make it only halfway. It just reminds me how much stronger Barb's ex is than me.

Then I remember what I came down here for and gently put the weapon back. There's the porcelain baby Jesus, lying in a porcelain manger. I grab it and shine my way back up the stairs.

"This is a first," Barb says, twisting some lights around the pine tree.

"What's that?"

"Trimming a real tree. Tony always used to haul up the fake one. He hates this smell."

"I love it," I say, inhaling deeply. "How can anyone not like the smell of pine needles?"

"I told you, he's a psycho."

"Speaking of which," I say, "I noticed the crossbow in the basement."

"It's still there? He took a bunch of weapons when I kicked him out. He must have forgotten it."

I rewind to earlier that day, Tony pulling me out of the car. He could have killed me. He might have been packing.

"I'm sure he's going to be thrilled when he finds out I was trimming this tree with you."

"I'm sure the neighbors are gossiping right now,"

she says. "I've gone out of my mind with grief and now I'm sleeping with some weirdo."

"Thanks," I say as she gives me a quick kiss on the cheek.

I reach down and plug in the strand of lights. When I stand up, Barb's giving me a sheepish smile.

"What now?"

"Can I ask you a favor?" she says, pinching her forefinger and thumb together. "A little one?"

"Anything," I say.

"Would you take Jack to see Santa tomorrow? The nurse said he'll be strong enough to leave the hospital for a few hours. And you two haven't spent any time alone."

"Santa?" I say.

"There's one at the Warwick Mall."

"I'd love to take him," I say. If I *have* to, I think. If it's going to help me get laid tonight.

"Sorry about my outburst," Barb says. "I guess I was just lashing out."

After the tree is trimmed, I sit on the couch and Barb lies down, her legs over my knees. Taking sips from mugs of spiked eggnog, we watch the multicolored lights fade in and out.

"What time do you think it is?" she says.

"I don't know. Eight. Nine."

"I've got to go back to the hospital."

"What if he's asleep?" I say.

"Doesn't matter. It's just the thought of him lying there."

"But you're exhausted," I say, watching her put on her parka, pull on her boots. I stand up as well and try to pull myself together.

"Sleep in my bed upstairs," she says. "I'll be back in an hour."

I kiss her good-bye and sit on the couch, wondering if I should just hop in the Mazda and head back to New York. I could sign up for the skin cancer symposium with Dr. Tolson and try to find another Alex. I wouldn't even have to fake it now.

I listen to Barb's car door slam, watch the headlights flare on the living room curtain. But something's bothering me. Walking across the room, I peel the BUSH/CHENEY poster off the window and rip it in two. Then I feed it to the smoldering fire, watching the glossy posterboard eat itself. Tomorrow, I'll lower the stars and stripes. Maybe I got my ass kicked, but I won't back down. Reaching into the bin by the fireplace I pick up another log and gently place it on the spent one.

The phone is ringing again. I freeze in place until it stops. Then I pull the curtains closed, just in case Tony decides to take a shot at me with one of his weapons. I put a pillow over the phone and walk upstairs, flopping on the queen-size mattress. I'm just about to drift off when I hear the muffled ringing begin again.

How does he find the time? I wonder to myself, picturing Tony holding the receiver to his ear, praying that Barb will just pick up. His throat loaded with words he'll never get to use. I lecture him in my sleepy mind. I tell him she's going to have a nervous breakdown. I tell him he doesn't really love his son, because he wouldn't act like this. He wouldn't waste this precious time.

I'm startled awake four hours later, when Barb finally comes home. Tosses the keys on the kitchen table. I hear her open the refrigerator, lift the cap off a beer. She kicks off her shoes, turns on the television, turns it off. I realize she must be even more agitated then before. She's walking slowly up the stairs now. I can see the vague shape of her body in the doorway, hear the slosh of beer as the bottle is lifted to her lips. For a long time, we just stare at each other in the darkness, waiting for each other's faces to come into focus.

"I'm not going to have sex with you," she finally says. "So don't even ask."

To be honest, my day of male bonding with Jack doesn't get off to a great beginning. For starters, I woke up this morning and, thanks to Barb, felt absolutely terrified about the fact that I'm going to die. I lay awake on a strange bed and none of the old mental defenses seemed to work. It just washed over me, taking courage and one-step-at-a-time and even some vague idea of a possible afterlife with it. By the time I'd thrown off the blanket and walked into the bathroom, the wave of fear had rolled on. I stared down at my white belly as I peed, felt the cold tiles under my feet, frowned at myself in the mirror, and gradually I felt more or less like myself again. All the same, when I pick Jack up at the hospital, I'm in a lousy mood.

For a kid who's just undergone a one-week course of chemotherapy, Jack's in a pretty sunny frame of mind. As I drive the Durango to the Warwick Mall, he kicks his sneakers up against the dashboard and has a long conversation with himself about the four hospital nurses who are in love with him. He interrupts himself only to tell me when I have to make a right or a left.

"Right at the next light," he says, hugging his knees and waving to some lady stuck in the crosswalk. "I don't want to hurt Mandy's feelings, that's the problem. Because I can tell that Becca likes me even more. 'Cause they once had a fight over who was going to give me a sponge bath. *This* light. You seem really distracted today. Is everything all right?"

"Everything's fine," I say, turning onto Bald Hill Road. I can see the hangarlike mall looming in the distance. "Back to your sponge bath."

"Anyway," Jack says, slapping his knee importantly. "Mandy's more beautiful than Becca, but Becca has nicer eyes. And I already told her that she's my favorite nurse."

"Sounds complicated," I say, taking the exit ramp too fast. The centrifugal force pushes Jack toward me. For a moment, he's forced to lean against me. I straighten out and speed down the highway.

"That's the mall," Jack says. "You're going too fast."

"Really?" I say, giving him a fake confused look. "Thanks for pointing it out."

"Anyway," Jack says, staring out the passenger window and picking up where he left off. If I weren't so preoccupied, I might indulge the whole Becca and Mandy love triangle, but the truth is I'm having a very hard time playing along. By the time I reach the parking lot, I've completely lost track of his show-off fantasy love life, not that my attention really matters. He's mostly talking to himself. It's his world, and I'd have to be a real asshole to puncture it. So I just sit there and wait for him to finish.

"Ready for Santa?" I say.

For a good half hour, Jack and I glide up and down escalators, revisit the information kiosk twice, take a breather by the indoor waterfall, and still can't manage to find Santa.

"This is ridiculous," Jack says.

"He's on the B concourse," I say, looking at an obelisk that contains a map of the four floors. "Follow me."

Again, we glide toward the blazing skylight, sailing through undying rubbery leaves and away from the tiny pennies in the wishing pool beneath us. About four escalator steps from the top, that wave hits me again. I grab the handrail, carefully step off, and flop down in the nearest chair by the food court.

"Paul," Jack says, watching me from a distance. "Are you okay?"

"I'm fine," I say, staring at my shoes, waiting for it to pass. I'm going to die, and I'm stuck in a mall, looking for Santa. My brain can't combine these two realities. One of them must be impossible.

"Maybe it's your meds," Jack says, trying to be helpful.

"I'm not taking any meds," I say. "Listen. Can you just shut up for a second?"

I say this loudly enough that four passing families seem to stop at once. I can hear them mumbling to themselves and then one another, as if they were pondering more direct action.

"Okay, let's go," I say, finally looking up. But Jack, of course, is gone. I ask the family lingering by the escalator if they've seen in which direction he went.

"Through the Sunglass Hut," the dad says with disgust, shaking his mop of gray hair at me and ushering his little boy away.

It takes me another fifteen frantic minutes to find Jack. Hearing screaming kids, I follow the noise into the Disney Store, where a security guard disguised as Minnie Mouse is keeping children and parents in a tightly packed line.

"Where do you think you're going?" a mother asks me angrily as I step forward.

"I'm looking for my son," I say, to her and anyone else who will listen. "He's wearing a Minnesota Vikings cap?"

"The boy with the bald head," her little girl offers.

"Oh," she says, instant sympathy clouding her face. "They let him go to the front."

I bow my head and mumble apologies all the way up the line, which snakes through two aisles before I finally see Santa's Workshop come into view.

"Finding my son, finding my son," I say, a little mantra that gets me all the way to Santa, and Jack, who's smiling at me from his knee, pleased at the special treatment he lives for. Cap in his hand. Bald head shining under the tiny Santa spotlights.

"Are you feeling better, Paul?" Jack says from his perch.

"Yes," I say, as a line of anxious kids looks on. "I'm feeling much better now."

"Paul has cancer," Jack says to the Santa, who furrows his cotton-clad eyebrows in genuine shock, and then, thankful to be Santa, quickly ushers the troublesome kid off his fat red leg before he shares another secret.

Back in the truck, I decide it's time to have the Talk.

"Jack," I say, "You've got to stop doing that."

"What?"

"Taking off your hat so you can cut lines."

"Paul?"

"Yeah."

"Just because you drove me to the mall doesn't mean you get to be my father. Can you please get me back to the hospital? I'm feeling kind of nauseous."

"No," I say, staring out the windshield at the sliding doors of the mall. The opening, the closing, the customers momentarily dazed by the blast of winter sunlight. I sit there until the silence starts to make Jack uncomfortable.

"I'm sorry," he says. "Okay? Can we go now?"

I wonder if I can tell him exactly how I feel. I wonder if adults are even allowed to do that with kids.

"Jack," I say. "I think you and me are a lot alike."

" 'Cause we're both sick."

"No," I say. "Not just because of that. I think we see things the same way."

I decide to keep the part about how amazingly selfish we both are to myself. Because Jack has the right to be. He's a kid, and he'd probably grow out of it, if he had the chance.

Jack's looking at me now, waiting for me to finish having this conversation with myself.

I put the car in drive and head back to the hospital.

The phone is ringing again, under the pillow, but Barb ignores it, as usual. I've been embellishing my day with Jack, making it sound a whole lot more successful than it was. We're lying on the sofa in the living room.

"Why don't we just disconnect it?" I say.

"Because then I wouldn't know if he stopped calling," she says. "And when he stops calling that means he'll probably take it to the next level. Hopefully by then, me and Jack won't be around."

"It's one in the morning," I say. "What could he possibly have to say to you?"

"The same old thing," she says. "He'll tell me how happy he is. How smart his girlfriend is. How much sex they have. It's his way of telling me he can't live without me."

There's a brief silence, and then the phone begins ringing again.

"You know what?" I say, still burning from the humiliating push-around in the Wal-Mart parking lot. "I'm going to answer it."

"Paul," she says, giving me a worried look. "I really don't think you want to do that."

But it's too late. The receiver's in my hand and I've got something to say.

"Tony," I say, a lump of sarcastic pleasure caught in my throat. "Don't you think it's time to move on?"

But all I hear is bristling silence. I slam the phone back down in its cradle.

"Come here, tough guy," Barb says, raising the blanket. I crawl under it and she flaps it around my shoulder, pulls me closer. Then a long wet kiss.

"It hit me by the way," I say to her.

"What did?"

"The fact that I'm going to die. I couldn't get back to sleep this morning."

"Oh Paul," she says, genuinely sorry. "That's terrible."

"It's all right," I say. "I guess it was inevitable. I'll tell you one thing, though. Anyone who says it makes life sweeter is full of shit. It just makes you feel like you're beside the point."

I'm thinking of Alex, sitting on that park bench, amused at how she once thought she was the center of the universe. I still have her credit card in my wallet, the one she left on the table at Per Se before running away to max out her life. I never saw her again.

"Makes you feel powerless," Barb says.

"Exactly," I say. "I always felt, not God necessarily,

but *something*, was looking out for me. I mean *at* me. Like some invisible force was keeping an eye on me every day. Not like influencing my existence or anything, but just *aware* of it. There goes Paul, here he comes again. Another day in the books. See you tomorrow. But there's no one there. There's no invisible force getting all rattled because I might cease to exist."

"I'm here," she says. "If that counts at all."

She kisses me again, and I let the subject drop. I want to let it drop forever. Who wants to think about being wiped off the face of the earth?

We have sex for the first time since Minneapolis, and to tell you the truth, it feels odd at first because Jack isn't around. There's no reason to feel guilty or rushed or anything. And maybe because of that, it's tentative, apologetic, groping. As if, on the verge of real intimacy, we're scared of offending each other. There's too much at stake.

"No," she says, hooking her calves around my back when I start to pull out. "Stay inside me."

I wake up a few hours later. I'm freezing, even underneath the blanket. Not wanting to wake her up by turning on the light, I find the flashlight and click it on. A little unsteady still, I weave toward the fireplace and find the steel poker. But jabbing at the charred logs produces only a few thin sparks. I find myself looking at the backs of several framed photographs on the mantelpiece. After kicking Tony out of the house, Barb must have turned them toward the wall. I aim the beam at each of them, my sleepy brain trying to adjust to this information.

Tony, hands on hips, pretending to be impressed by Old Faithful.

Tony, hands on hips, watching a much younger Jack feed some rabid looking goat at a petting zoo.

Tony, hands on hips, standing next to Barb, at the base of a tall waterfall.

It's as if a cardboard cutout of Tony had been pasted onto each photograph. The man has one pose. And probably one expression. But I can't see his eyes because they're covered by Oakley sunglasses in each snapshot. I almost feel sorry for the guy.

"No wonder she left him," I say, shining the flashlight out the bay window, where cuticles of ice have formed on the panes.

I'm starving. The kind of starving you get only when you're sleeping in someone else's house. Lured by the promise of unknown foods, and realizing I haven't had a decent meal in more than a day, I flick on the kitchen light and wait for it to catch. But first things first, I think, looking down at my pale, naked legs. My glazed dick framed in the fly of my boxers. I tuck it back in.

It isn't until I actually open the refrigerator that I realize someone is watching me from the darkened breakfast nook. Because the moonlight is catching on the dial of this person's watch, and further along are his clenched knuckles, four patches of short black hair on each finger.

"Help yourself," Tony says softly.

"Holy shit," I say. "You scared me."

I realize how odd this sounds. As if he hadn't meant to.

"Make yourself a sandwich," he says. "Then come and sit down."

I've made a lot of sandwiches in my life. But I've never made a sandwich in front of a man after screwing his ex-wife. And I do my best. I take out two pieces of whole-wheat bread. I spread on a little mayo. I put it on a plate, and then I sit down. I don't want to seem greedy.

"There's cold cuts," Tony says, reaching above him and pulling the light chain.

"I'm fine," I say, looking down at my hands, which seem to be a light year away from picking up the lousiest sandwich ever made.

"Pickles," he says. "Get yourself a few pickles. That's a pathetic sandwich."

"I'm not even hungry, really," I say, forcing myself to look up. And the expression I had to guess at in all those photographs of Tony on the mantelpiece is finally revealed to me. How can I put it? He seems bored. His eyes seemingly more interested in the reflection of the light on his watch than the stranger in his house. It's only with great effort that he raises his chin and forces himself to look at me. And what he sees seems to bore him even more. Because I'm no match. I don't even have the guts to eat a mayonnaise sandwich.

"Jack tells me you have cancer," he says. "Is that true?"

"Actually," I say, gripping my plate with both hands and then steering it to the right, as if I were trying to drive somewhere. "It's a funny thing. I didn't. And then it turns out I do. And I just haven't been acting like myself. Thus . . . "

Thus. A good word. Almost biblical sounding and holy. I raise my hands as if the whole situation was beyond my control.

"So there's really no point in killing you," he says.

"Not really," I say. "I'm a goner. I'm history, basically. I'm just playing out the string."

I watch him twist his wrist slightly, then tilt his head. There's the sound of air being slowly forced from his nostrils as he looks down at his thick watch. It's as if he's waiting for a real human being to come walking into this kitchen, not the phantom who happened to stumble in.

"Listen," he says politely. "I've got to run. But I want you to relay a message to my wife. I'd tell her myself. But she's not picking up the phone, and when I see her in public she tends to throw things at me."

"I'm happy to," I say.

"The message," he says, standing up, gripping my shoulder, and almost touching his thick, chapped lips to my ear, "is that Jack is going to be spending Christmas with my girlfriend and me. You'll tell her?"

"Absolutely," I say.

"Good. Because if you don't, I'm going to come back here tomorrow night and I'm going to kill you. Even if you do have cancer. Enjoy your sandwich."

With that, he turns and slowly walks out of his former kitchen, gently kicking open the door in a familiar way and pulling the sides of his fleece jacket snug over his shoulders. Through the open door I can see that silver BMW, that woman with the tall red hair sitting in the driver's seat, fast asleep.

# CHAPTER 16

BLUE GREASE FILTERS through cold winter sunlight. The smell of meat crackling and snapping in a heavy pan. Nothing in the world like waking up to the sound of breakfast already half made. I stretch my arms out and groan. Barb steps into the room and kicks one of my feet playfully. She's wearing a faded green apron and she's tied her hair back, and if the day ended here, I could be happy forever, but no, I have to ruin everything. My mind alerts me to the fact that, even as I'm smiling back at her, there won't be too many more breakfasts like this for Paul Mauro. And why me? Why isn't it you? How terrifying it is when I realize I'll enjoy only so many more glasses of freshly squeezed orange juice. That I'll probably make it through only a gallon of maple syrup. A few more pounds of bacon. And I feel completely healthy as I sit down at the kitchen table. I feel ten times healthier than anyone I know.

"I see you had a midnight snack," Barb says, unstringing her apron and joining me at the table.

Weird dream, I tell myself. Is it possible it was just a dream?

"Barb," I say, rubbing my face and trying to concentrate. This is going to come as a shock to her.

"Tony was here," she says, with a wild-eyed look.

"Yes," I say. "He was sitting right here. He scared the hell out of me."

"What did he want?"

"I thought he was going to kill me."

"What did he say?"

But before I even get the third word of Tony's special message out of my mouth, Barb's shoved her arms into her white parka and she's out the door. I grab a single piece of bacon and follow her.

Jack, of course, is gone. Tony and his girlfriend have even taken the stuffed animals from the windowsill. But they've left the useless key to the town of Coventry. I stuff it in my pocket, because it looks depressing sitting there by itself. Barb is out in the hallway screaming at some nurse, asking her how on earth they could discharge a kid who was in a chemo cycle.

"His father kept saying how much he just wanted him home for Christmas," the nurse says meekly.

Barb storms back into the room and stares at the newly made bed, touching the tight hem of the newly changed sheet. I don't say anything at all. Tony might not find it worth the effort to kill me, but I have the feeling that if I say the wrong thing right now, Barb will kick my teeth out.

"What are we going to do?"

I want to tell her that I'm the wrong person to ask. After all, if I hadn't shown up with that scraggly Christmas tree, maybe her ex wouldn't have decided it was time to raise the stakes.

"I'll come up with something," I say, hugging her. "Trust me. Jack'll be home for Christmas."

Barb's crying, but I can't see, because my chin is resting on her head. It's like she's already mourning Jack, the empty space he's left behind. If it's this bad now, I wonder, what's going to happen when he dies? Or is this the worst part, when the child she loves is alive? It must seem to her like love only proves how useless it is. It laces up pillow-sized boxing gloves and swings away, protecting no one. It can't even keep a sick kid in the hospital.

I don't wait for dawn this time. As soon as Barb falls asleep upstairs, I sit at the kitchen table and write her a note:

*Barb,*

*I know you're going to be angry with me,*
*but I have to leave. It seems like when I*
*arrive on the scene, everything just gets*
*worse. I'm adding to your misery. And*
*I'm definitely not helping the situation.*
*Please give Jack a big hug for me.*

> *Love you both and*
> *Merry Christmas,*
>
> *Paul*

Merry Christmas? I erase these two words and blow away the pink bits of rubber, but the shadow of the thought is still legible, so I crumple the note and begin again. By the time I get my exit strategy right, the wastebasket is filled with fist-sized balls of paper, because every word seems false, and falseness is the last thing that's called for now. Finally, I scratch out:

*Barb,*

*I'm a self-serving asshole. I deserve to*
*die. Be thankful I'm out of your hair.*

> *Love,*
>
> *Paul*

• • •

Christmas Eve. And where does the man who's running out of time find himself?

At a strip club in Providence, Rhode Island, staring at Santa's pierced clit.

Not Santa exactly, but the coffee-colored girl who's wearing his hat. Who's been performing for my pleasure for the last ten minutes. Why not? I've already handed her six twenty-dollar bills. The other customers, mostly Mexican day-labor types and a handful of frat boys from Boston, do their best to get an angle and occasionally glare at me jealously. The bouncer by the door, in his dandruff-specked black turtleneck, is just looking for a reason to kick me out. The stripper plays with herself and blows a kiss to someone in the DJ booth. Then she turns over on her stomach and raises her ass in the air. I'm looking at an upside-down face. Alarmingly green eyes.

I reach out and the bouncer takes a few steps forward. He relaxes when he sees I'm just handing her another twenty. Her fingers dance like the bristles of an anemone, catching the bill and quickly tucking it underneath her G-string.

Since I've given her so much money in so little time, she can't avoid looking a little suspicious. Or maybe it's the blank expression on my face.

"So," she says, kneeling, waiting for the next song

to begin, "did you get all your Christmas shopping done?"

"Yeah," I lie. "Just in time."

"I bet you spoil everyone," she says, raising her arms as "Ship of Fools" begins to play.

"I love this song," I say, watching her dance. "It's just so melancholy when you hear it at a strip club."

"You're feeling melancholy?" she says, drawing the corners of her mouth down.

"A little," I say.

"Why's that?" she says, turning her head and waving to an Asian guy who's just walked in.

"Well," I say. "It's Christmas Eve and I just ran away from the only two people I love."

But she never hears my confession. She's too distracted by the Asian guy.

"Hey James," she says to him.

James unzips his leather jacket and whips off his sunglasses, like he's Knight Rider or something. It pisses me off because she was really getting into "Ship of Fools," and now she's already shimmying over to him and he's snapping his fingers at the cocktail waitress, and I want my perfect moment, melancholy or otherwise. I've got plenty of cash on me, but I'm running out of time.

"Thanks," I shout at the girl. "And by the way, I'm dying of cancer."

The next thing I know she's looking at the bouncer and pointing at me. He takes about a half second to reach me and yank me out of my seat.

"Do you know how many times she's heard that?" he says to me, pushing me out of the club. "We should put a sign on the wall."

"Please just let me hear the end of this song," I shout over the music. "I'll stand by the door."

"Buy the CD," he says, pushing me out the metal door. "You can listen to it as much as you want."

Outside, in the small parking lot that the club shares with a shuttered store, snow has begun to fall. On the factories. On the cars. On the graveyards, wherever they are. On this gigantic blue termite that sits on the roof of Northeast Pest Control. I put my car keys back in my pocket and climb up a slippery steel ladder bolted to the side of the building. A minute later, out of breath, I'm threading my way through a line of cracked, dirty skylights.

You've never really seen the city of Providence at night, trust me, until you've seen it from the point of view of a gigantic metal termite wrapped in blinking Christmas lights. The white headlights of traffic streaming toward Boston below. The red brake lights streaming toward New York. The snow sinking into the black highway. And the termite, lording it over everything.

"What are you waiting for?" I ask the bug, gripping one of his cold, steel legs. Easy to imagine him slipping down the other side of the building in a heartbeat. Causing a ten-car pileup. Pausing to clean his massive antennae somewhere near Bridgeport. I pat him on his midsection and his hollowness comes ringing back to me. What can he do? Another typical example of the human race. They build the ultimate predator and then nail him to a fucking factory roof so he can only salivate over rush hour.

Clambering back down the steel ladder, I lose my balance on the third rung and land awkwardly on my ankle.

"Shit," I say, clutching it, my right hand covered with freezing snow. I look up and see two people in the front seat of the Toyota Camry parked next to my Mazda. As I limp to my car, I realize it's the stripper and Knight Rider, his eyes pressed closed in ecstasy as she gives him a handjob and pretends not to notice me.

I climb into the Mazda, letting it warm up, trying not to look to my right, though I can vaguely tell that things are winding down. I turn on my headlights, pinning two out-of-focus circles on the brick wall of Northeast Pest Control and its faded, very un-catchy slogan, "We Bug Bugs!"

Ruminating on this, I ease out of the lot. Though the interstate hums a hundred yards away, it seems to take me an hour to find the on ramp. And then I'm headed back in the wrong direction, back toward Coventry, that stupid blue termite staring at me in my rearview mirror, the sky already a shade lighter than its metal skin. And it's talking to me. Even a giant termite thinks it should give me advice.

"Save Christmas," it says, its bug voice rattling the inside of my car. "It's the least you can do."

# CHAPTER 17

CHRISTMAS HAS NEVER been my favorite holiday. It always seems so deserted, and never more so than here, parked outside Barb's house on Hollyhock Lane. It's possible to imagine I'm the only human being who exists for miles.

Despite the fact that Jack is spending Christmas at Tony's house, Barb has finished putting up the decorations. There's a mistletoe reindeer standing on the front lawn, and a fringed banner stretched across the living-room window that says HAPPY HOLIDAYS. Inside, I can see the multicolored lights on the tree, winking out and in, thread by thread.

The front door is open, just the way I left it. Barb must still be asleep. I walk through the kitchen and find my pathetic note on the table. I crumple it up and add it to the other balls of paper in the wastebasket, then I sneak into the living room.

Barb has laid out all of Jack's presents. A whole stack of them almost obliterate the tree. There's even one with my name on it. I pick it up and open the small card.

"For Paul," it says inside. "A really nice guy. Love, Jack and Barb."

Funny how the old Paul caught up to me. After all those miles I put between us, and the lies to throw him off my trail, suddenly I'm right back where I started. It says it right there on the card.

I get down on one knee and carefully lay the gift on the other boxes. I'm not done yet. I just might surprise you.

Standing up again, I see that the photographs of Tony on the mantelpiece have been removed, and that Barb has hung three red stockings, which bulge with gifts. Even if she's hidden his photographs, I know that Tony's still going to ruin Barb's Christmas. And to tell you the truth, it really pisses me off. I can tell she's put her heart into this. And I have also, lugging that tree all the way from Sunset Park. For all I know, it might be my last Christmas, too.

I look at the tree and picture the three of us sitting around in our pajamas, handing one another gifts, pecking one another on the cheek, building a fire. The thought of it actually makes me happy.

It must be nine o'clock already. I wince when I think of Jack at his father's house. What he's in for with those relatives. The hundred times they'll ask him to smile. The pointless gifts they'll push on him.

I walk down to the basement, thinking of Tony and how he'll do his best to ruin Barb's life. Above all, he'll waste her time.

I dust off the crossbow with the heel of my hand and inspect it by the flat light of the casement window.

I hook my index finger on the steel wire and try to pull it back, but it doesn't budge. I look at the red indentation it's left on my fingertip and start kicking away the shrouded toys on the floor, searching for something that resembles an arrow.

Tony has a nice house, which doesn't surprise me, with a long curvy driveway. At the end of it, I can distinctly make out the three-story colonial, with its cupola and brick chimneys, patio, covered pool, and a wreath on the enormous front door. Driving my Mazda to the house is out of the question. So I park the car on the shoulder of the road and reach for the knapsack in the backseat. Just in case someone thinks I've abandoned the car, I hit the hazards.

I've never been hunting in my life, let alone for humans, on Christmas, with a crossbow.

No, that isn't completely true. Once, my father dragged me out to watch him try to shoot some quail. I remember ducking his shotgun, which he seemed to be training on me half the time. And come to think of it, I remember that we spent the night at a motel on the way back and that I had a separate room, which I thought was great, until I heard the sound of my father groaning through the wall. I don't know if that was number 432 or 512. He was pretty old then. And I don't know why the fuck I'm thinking of this now, as I gingerly step over these dead leaves, hiding behind the trunk of a bare maple tree.

Forgive him, a voice says. Forgive everybody while you're at it! Let's go back to the strip club. Let's while away the last of our days in murmur-filled bars. Let's order a Rusty Nail and pretend we're someone else. Let's drive until we find some seaside town, some shithole just seedy enough to really cheer you up. Let's sit on a crescent of thin sand and watch the sun glint off the cold ocean. Turn up our collar and smile at the Tilt-a-Wheel frozen in place. Let's find an old hotel where they don't have cable, or Internet, or anything. Where it's possible that your own bad news will never find you.

But I ignore this somewhat shrill voice, and I run toward the next tree, dry leaves crunching under my sneakers, a thin layer of snow dusting the underbrush. To tell you the truth, I should have done this sooner, because it's a great distraction. My heart's going batshit. Always the last to know, it wants to know what in fuck is going on.

I'm at the terrace now. The red bricks. I'm walking past the little colored jockey, holding out his lantern. I'm pressing the bell.

I'm pressing the bell!

I unzip the knapsack. I take out the crossbow, delicately place an arrow in the notch, then step on the front of the weapon while pulling upward with a grunt. A half inch away from locking in place, the steel wire starts to tremble and then my whole arm starts to shake. I pull so hard I think my asshole is going to pop out, but the steel string finally locks in place. It's armed.

But no one answers the door. Christmas morning, what do you expect? It's all about yawning and turning back over, mashing a pillow over an ear.

We bug bugs, I repeat to myself. That silly slogan.

But it's true. This has to be done.

I press the bell for ten seconds. Wait. Press it for another thirty. This time I know someone's moving. I don't hear it. I see it. The windowpane to my right vibrates slightly.

And then nothing.

I can run away. Absolutely nothing has happened. I could leave the crossbow right here. He forgot it anyway. I'm just returning it. And besides, am I really going to die? Because if there's the slightest chance I might survive cancer, then this is a really bad move.

I'm shaking. I've always been a shaker. It makes

sense that my body would go to pieces now. I must look like I have cerebral palsy. Even my face is acting up. The eyebrows. The lips. The teeth.

Shivering like an idiot, I retreat to the metal lawn jockey, Tony's own little nigger, and get down on one knee, thinking, This is definitely one more reason to evict Tony from the planet. And then, while I'm on a roll, maybe I'll avenge every other lawn jockey in New England. I rest the crossbow on the statue's outstretched arm. His white pupils make him look even more alarmed.

I tell myself I can handle this.

The door opens and Tony instantly fills the space. He's wearing leather slippers and blue pajamas, mono-grammed with his initials. A cold bit of wind licks at the hem of his silk robe.

"Who is it?" a voice asks from inside.

"No one," he says, taking a few quick steps toward me and reaching out for the crossbow, scratching the air impatiently with his fingers.

Then they go stiff.

I realize I've pulled the trigger because the cross-bow has lost all its tension. I look and see the bolt has sunk into Tony's leather slipper, a puff of concrete dust sailing across the terrace. It's happened so fast that the expression on Tony's face hasn't yet changed. He still looks irritated, but maybe not quite as confident as before. As he drags his slipper toward me, I can hear the point of the arrow rasping against the bricks. We both watch as blood wells up in his slipper and begins to spread around his heel.

"You shot me," he says, leaning over and patting the air around the bolt, as if he were afraid to touch it.

"I had to," I say.

But he's turned his back. He's turned his back and he's dragging his impaled slipper back to the house, walking sideways and grunting each time he takes a step. I stand up and follow him as he slowly opens the door.

I've stopped shaking. I've stopped thinking. I'm only following, taking it one step at a time as Tony tries to close the door behind him. But he's too weak now. I push it open with a finger and follow him into his den, where the Christmas presents have been assembled in front of an imposing, perfectly conical tree. Big ticket items: a ten-speed bike, a giant LCD TV, a putting green. He leads me right to the foot of the cantilevered staircase, where his girlfriend stands on a froth of white carpet, tightening the belt of her purple bathrobe and giving me a slightly concerned look before turning toward him.

"Tony," she says, leaning over. "What's in your foot? Why are you making that funny face?"

I leave the two of them together and start making my way upstairs, aware that Tony has crashed to the ground behind me. The impact of his body sends shock waves all the way up the stairs.

Now I'm in the kids' room. A bunk bed. A screen-saver on the computer showering green and blue sparks. I pull the yellow blanket off the top bunk and realize it's not Jack. It's the girlfriend's son. Dropping to a knee, I pull the cover off the sleeping boy in the lower bunk and remember that my mother always said you have to wake a child gently, otherwise they'll ruin your whole morning.

"Jack," I whisper. "Jack."

He blinks his eyes open, lifts his head off the saliva-soaked pillow. A darker blue circle on dark blue. He doesn't say a word. Instead he raises himself up, as if he were doing a sit-up, and falls on me, his arms loosely hanging on my neck, and instantly goes to sleep again.

"Jack," I say.

"What," he murmurs against my arm.

"How fast can you get dressed?"

By the time Jack and I walk downstairs, Tony is lying on the carpet, near the winking Christmas tree, yelling orders at his girlfriend.

"How much blood am I losing?" he says, to her, me, Jack, anybody.

"I'm getting a cold pack," his girlfriend shouts from the kitchen. "The ambulance is on its way. Oh my God."

She's standing in the hallway, holding the blue cold pack against her chest. I'm staring down at Tony.

"How much blood?" he says to me.

"You'll survive," I say. "But if you ever take Jack again I'm going to come back here and kill you."

"Get out of here," he spits at me, shielding his face at the same time, just in case I might have another weapon on me.

"Let's go," I say to Jack, dragging him by his hand and leading him out the door.

"What's going on?" he says as I give him a push on the terrace. We're jogging across the frozen lawn now, but Jack can't stop asking me the same question. What is it about kids? They take an hour to put on a sneaker the wrong way and then they run into walls when you're asking for lickety-split. Jack's fallen to the ground. He's not exactly in the greatest shape to begin with, and here we are running the sixty-yard dash.

I jog back toward him and pick him up off the ground, snow mashed against his wool sweater.

"Did Dad hurt himself?" Jack says, trying to catch his breath.

"Something like that. Come on, we're almost there."

"Shouldn't we wait for the ambulance?"

"I'm sure they'll be fine," I say, ripping my car keys out of my jeans' pocket and promptly losing them in midair. They drop somewhere behind me and I freeze.

"What happened?" Jack says. "How come we're running anyway?"

"Jack," I say, trying to remain calm. "Stop asking me questions. Help me find my fucking keys."

"You said *fuck*."

"You're right," I say. "I shouldn't curse."

Because it's not too late to be a good role model. And it's Christmas.

As we get down on our hands and knees, turning over frozen leaves, we can hear screams in the distance. Tony's girlfriend is hysterical, her voice ricocheting off everything. It seems like when it gets cold, all of nature shrinks to the size of someone's living room.

We can hear every word. I shot her boyfriend. Someone help please. I'm going to get her next.

I have no interest in getting her, or her fat son. I'm trying to find my car keys. I'm still pawing at the ground, but I can feel Jack glaring at me.

"You shot my dad," he says softly.

"He deserved it," I say quietly. I've already resolved to be very matter of fact about this. We're going to enjoy Christmas. I've made a big effort this year.

Jack isn't looking for my keys anymore. He's sitting on the snow, touching his eyes. Coughing and sobbing. His mouth wrenched open.

At the same time I'm looking at him, I catch sight

of one of my keys. I reach out and pull them from the dirt.

"Let's go," I say.

"I'm not going with you," he says, tearing his hand away from mine. I crouch next to him.

"Jack," I say. "I want to tell you something. I'm not going to hold back."

He takes his hand away from his eyes and sniffles. I want to hug him, but I have to get this over with first.

"We're going to die. Both of us."

"*You're* going to die," Jack says, standing up. He starts to run away, but he doesn't get far. I've got him in a bear hug, terrified that I'll lose him. I see myself doing this. I hate myself for doing this. What if he's right? What if I'm just trying to drag him down to the grave with me?

I pull him to the ground. His fingernails are dug into my arm. He's trying to bite my wrist.

"Jack," I say. "They don't love you. You can't go back."

He screams then. A real scream that shakes every last bird from the branches above us. I'm still looking at myself now. I'm looking at myself hugging a screaming kid, and I'm thinking, I've got to be right. I'm betting it all on this one moment. And the truth is, I can't be sure. I'm just going on instinct now. A wave of love. It's a whole lot better than fear. In fact, I don't care how far it carries me.

"We love you Jack," I say. "Me and your mom. We have to make the most of it. You know what I'm saying? We can't waste any more time."

I feel his body relax, just a little.

"I'm going to let you go," I whisper into his ear. "Are you going to come with me?"

"Okay," he says.

I let him go. I press my hands down into the snow and watch him run back toward the house. I can hear Tony's girlfriend screaming at him, asking him if he's all right. She's on the portable phone with the cops.

I'm telling myself I should get on my feet and get out of here. But all I can do is watch Tony's girlfriend wrap her arm around Jack and pull him back toward the house. I've started to walk back to my car, when I hear her voice again.

"Jack," she shouts.

When I turn he's already run across the terrace. He jumps the last three steps and nearly does another faceplant on the snowy lawn.

"Wait," he shouts at me.

It's been a long time since one word has made me this happy. And it's not the kind of word I thought I'd ever want to hear again. Because I don't have time to wait for anything anymore, and neither does Jack.

• • •

One of these days I'm going to write down what I've learned. Wise words for the children of tomorrow. And top on that list is going to be a whole subcategory titled "Think Ahead." Because when you don't think ahead, you're screwed.

Now, I don't have the heart to tell Barb as she kneels next to Jack and watches him open that Christmas present that I'm operating on a fairly limited time schedule. And even Jack knows this, he's white as chalk. But we're both making her nervous, and this bothers me, because she was ecstatic when I showed up with Jack. I told her that I'd had a man-to-man with Tony and that Jack was hers for the whole day.

"Well," I say, clapping my hands together, distinctly aware of the sound of approaching sirens.

They sound different in a small town. Just a steady whelping. Not bunched up and irregular, like they are in New York City, where you can always rest assured that at any given time, a whole bunch of people have it worse than you.

Here, it seems, I'm definitely going to be the star of the show. I'm the guy who has it worse than me.

"I'm out of here," I say.

Barb looks crushed. Jack's ripped open the red wrapping paper covering the Xbox, but he's not even looking at it. I've already ruined the moment.

"I want to go with him," he says.

"Why are you in such a hurry?" she says to me. "Can you please just be happy where you are just for once?"

"I know what you mean," I say. "And I wish I could. Jack will explain. After I'm gone."

"Paul shot Dad with a crossbow," Jack says, looking at his mother sadly, and fearfully, too, as if she might scream in astonishment, much as she hated Tony.

"I said *after* I'm gone," I shout at him, grabbing my keys off the kitchen table and walking out into the front yard. I turn to Barb as she follows me out and stands on the snow-covered concrete step, her breath visible. Her blond hair has fallen over her eyes. Her nightgown is wrinkled. I can see the blue veins stretched across her feet. I take a mental picture of Jack as he presses his temple against her thigh, the automatic way she squeezes his shoulder and keeps on staring at me. Not angry, but worried. And it's not perfect, but I don't want to leave.

"I love you," I shout at both of them. It's better than saying good-bye. Love lasts longer anyway. An hour, a day. Even after I'm gone, if it could just remain some-how, nosing around.

Fine, if you want to kill me, but let me come back as something else. Why would it bother you? If I could just be warm light on a winter day, passing through an icy window, painting their hands. This strange family that isn't even mine.

# CHAPTER 18

"HEARD ABOUT LEE?" Eric says, popping open a bottle of Martinelli Sparkling Cider. Terry's got him on the wagon. Nicotine patch on the arm. All the hard alcohol smashed and thrown away. But still, it's New Year's, couldn't she at least have waited until January 2?

"No," I say. "What's the latest?"

"They've already set a wedding date. But that's not even the big news."

I already know the big news, before he even tells me.

"Her mother died," I say.

"Yeah. How'd you know?"

"Because it figures I'd have to be tortured for five years about having kids and then Felipe would get all her mother's money."

"Anyway," Eric says, pouring me some cider, "money isn't everything, right?"

"I wonder what happened to Brenda," I say.

"Why don't you give her a ring? Where have you been anyway?"

I tell him that I've just driven down from Rhode Island.

I ask him if I can spend the night.

"Sure," he says. "But what's wrong with your apartment in Brooklyn?"

"Everything's in storage," I say, which is actually true, since the place is in Lee's name and she's already trying to sell it. But what I'm picturing is an unmarked police car, parked across the street, some detective just waiting for me to walk in. I'm not *that* stupid.

We walk back into the living room and flop onto the couch next to Terry, who's breastfeeding the little one again. I take a sip of the Martinelli and wish it were something stronger. Every second my mind keeps slipping back to the same old subject: Barb and Jack. Are they okay? Are they being hassled by detectives? Is even more of Jack's precious time being wasted? Have I just made things worse? And I keep kicking myself for what I told Jack in the woods. For Chrissakes, is that the way you talk to a kid with leukemia? I couldn't even get our biggest father-and-son moment right. Leave an arrow in Tony's foot and then tell Jack we're both going to die? There's no way around it. I'm not a father figure. I'm a sinkhole. Just like someone else.

"Nut never falls far from the tree," I say to Eric, nodding sagely.

"What?"

"We're just like Dad," I say. "We're selfish, twisted pricks. We're worthless."

Terry, squeezed between us, sighs disapprovingly and shrugs her breast back into the baby's mouth.

"Happy New Year to you, too," Eric says, raising his glass.

I clink his plastic champagne glass. Take a morose sip.

"You know what?" Eric says, turning to me with a reddening face. "Get the fuck out of my house."

"Oh, stop it!" Terry shouts, standing up. The baby whimpers and stares at us over her shoulder as she walks away, his powdery blue eyes widening in amazement. I understand.

"I didn't mean that," I say, staring at the decorations on their Christmas tree. A few strands of popcorn have turned yellow. A silvery foil spider has fallen to the ground. It can't crawl away.

"You did mean it," Eric says. "But that's all right. It's New Year's. Let's get drunk."

Outside, in the numbing cold, Eric steps on a mud-caked shovel and tries to dislocate some earth.

"You going to stand there watching the stars or help me?" he says.

"What are we digging up?" I say, taking the other smaller, child-sized spade. The one he bought for his son. The dirt is as hard as diamonds.

"Last year's Glenlivet," he says. "Uncle Ted gave it to me. I buried it out here, just in case it ever came to this."

"Came to what?" I say, watching the upstairs light being turned out. New Year's Eve and Terry's already going to sleep. It's not even nine o'clock.

"Being sober."

We work in silence for a few minutes, breathing hard over the shovels as they chuff into the ground and come away with thimblefuls of dirt. I might as well be digging with a spoon. But we get there. We have to.

"Careful now," Eric says, kneeling down. "Let me just wipe this off."

"I feel like an archaeologist," I say.

"I feel better already," Eric says, lifting out the bottle and flicking off a tiny, curling slug.

We retreat to the porch and take pulls off the dirty bottle, making pleased sounds as the twenty-five-year-old single malt rakes our throats.

"How is Uncle Ted?" I say.

"Dead."

I take another pull. It's too cold for false sympathy. Stick to the important things.

"I think I'm in love," I say.

What are they doing right now? They're both awake. I know that for sure. Maybe they're standing by my Christmas tree, holding sparklers, the white dashes flying through the air, Jack catching them painlessly with his hand.

"In love?" Eric says, turning toward me. He somehow manages to look pleased and jealous at the same time. "What's her name?"

"It's a family," I say.

"You're in love with a *family*?" he says, snatching the bottle angrily away from me.

"Kind of," I say, feeling wretched and complicated suddenly, as if my own body had internalized the whole wretched, complicated situation.

"That's weird," he says. "I thought you hated kids."

"I do," I say. "But this is an exception."

"So tell me more," he says.

And I do, as our fingers freeze off on the back porch. Eric, being a brother, knowing that I mean it this time, doesn't even go inside to take a leak, and I continue to tell him about Barb and Eric as he writes the first steaming letters of his name on the fence.

"I'm happy for you," he says, sitting back down and picking up the bottle again.

I watch him take another sip, wipe his lips. He hands me the bottle and then he puts his arm around my neck and pulls me toward him.

"You've got a good heart," he says, just beginning to sound a little buzzed. "Always did."

I dangle the bottle over the step, watching the liquid slosh inside. Then I hold it up to my eyes, squinting to read the label by the porch light.

"Twenty-five years old," I say. "How do we know it's not just ten or five?"

"Because it says twenty-five. Cask conditioned. Says it right there."

"Like we'd know the difference," I say, "It's the same color anyway." I let Eric pull the bottle away from me. He gives me a funny look and opens his mouth to say something, but then changes his mind.

"Tell me more about this weird family situation," he says. "How did you meet them?"

"I lied," I say, staring at the wooden fence. Pale light thrown off by the porch lamp showing the splinters. I realize there's no way around it. I have to tell him everything. Especially since the cops will probably be paying him a visit.

"Lied?"

"I told them I had cancer."

"Right," Eric says, lifting the bottle to his mouth. "Everyone knows you have cancer. So what's the lie part?"

I make my confession to the fence. It's easier not to look at Eric as I tell him how I'd seen my future sitting in my car in his driveway, and how I'd panicked and lied to Lee. I tell him about Alex and Brenda and Minnesota and Caneel Bay and Coventry and shooting Tony in the foot with an arrow. I keep looking at the fence and I wonder if Eric is going to let me keep on speaking or crack the bottle over my head. But he lets me tell the whole story. All I hear is the slosh of the Scotch as he takes another sip.

I'm done. It's freezing out here, but my face is flushed, as if the whole story had just bubbled out through my skin. He should say something. Or punch me. Or call the cops. All that's understandable. But not silence.

"What do you think?" I say, turning to him. Eric's eyelids have drifted a little lower. His lips are pursed and he's staring right back at me, shaking his head very slowly.

"That's truly pathetic," he says.

I reach for the bottle but he snaps it away from my hand, takes a gulp, then sets it on the porch. I watch him stand up.

"I'm sorry," I say to his leg.

"Really sad," he says, walking up the porch steps. Eric's right. I know he's right. But I'm already fuming. Who is he to judge me? He's probably ticked he didn't come up with the idea himself.

"Eric," I say.

"What?" he says, one hand on the screen door.

"You're a fucking coward," I say.

But this doesn't stop him either. He calmly twists the doorknob, steps inside, and closes it again. I just sit there, staring at the empty bottle of Scotch gleaming in the yard, mentally rewinding everything that just happened, to the part where Eric grabs me by the neck and tells me I have a good heart.

I'm too cold to really think about my next step. I suppose it's just a matter of finding the nearest police precinct and telling them I'm probably wanted in Rhode Island for the attempted murder of Tony's foot.

I hear the rubber of the door swishing open behind me.

"Don't worry," I say, turning toward Eric. "I'm leaving." He's already half-undressed, scratching the crotch of his plaid boxer shorts.

"Do me a favor," he says. "Bring in the bottle when you're done. Hide it under the couch. Then take it with you tomorrow."

New Year's Day. The heater in Eric's living room banging away. I'm lying under a pink Dora the Explorer quilt that doesn't even cover my feet. Staring through the windowpane at a square of cold blue sky.

I've been wide awake for hours, trying to make a decision, wondering how Eric can sleep so soundly upstairs with a fugitive crashing on his couch. I feel awful about what I said to him. I want to wake him up and tell him I didn't mean it. Tell him I love him. Tell him I really have cancer now, swear on my grave. But I figure that an early-morning confession won't go over too well with Terry. So I do the only thing I can do. I pull on my jeans, sweater, and parka. Splash some cold water on my face. Getting down on my knees, I reach for the empty Scotch bottle. I push open the front door, and close it as quietly as I can, like a thief in reverse. I crunch across the gravel, squinting down at my dirty sneakers. There's too much light, revealing too many imperfections. The cat turd on the front lawn. The rust on my car's roof. Opening the door, I toss the bottle in. Then I sit there and let the engine warm up, staring at the sun flashing on the dirty double-glazed windows of the house, the white metal blinds let down at a careless angle. If it weren't for this house, I'd still be married to Lee.

Run, the house says. Just like it did last time.

And I do.

# CHAPTER 19

I WON'T BORE you with the usual invalid crap. You've seen someone die, right? You're a grownup. The coughing. The aches. The sudden waves of exhaustion.

And I've been spending this year so badly.

Me, the one who should be maxing out every minute. Dancing in some wheatfield somewhere. Washing his thinning hair under a waterfall.

And where have I spent it?

Florida.

Jacksonville, Vilano Beach, St. Augustine, Titusville, Sebastian. Checking out of one mildewed motel room and into another, living on the money Eric wires me. I tell him I've changed my will, and that I'm going to pay him back, but he doesn't want to hear it. I don't think he really believes I have cancer now.

After I left my brother's place on New Year's Day, I drifted around Manhattan for a month before driving back north and checking into a motel in East Providence. I saw Barb one more time, but she came without Jack. I understood. I was, after all, a fugitive, and she hadn't completely forgiven me for ruining Christmas. I promised her I'd do the right thing and turn myself in. It was the courageous thing to say, and after we slept together, she made me swear I wasn't lying again.

But I didn't turn myself in. I drove to Boston and ditched the Mazda near South Station, then I took a bus to Florida.

In Fayetteville, I called Eric from a Roy Rogers and learned that the cops had indeed come looking for me. Though Eric made a point of telling me that they spent half the time snickering about my marksmanship.

In Savannah, I shed my parka and shoes. Bought a tropical short-sleeved shirt and a pair of flip-flops at a rest stop souvenir store. I squeezed my last hundred dollars for all it was worth, dining on Cheez-Its and trail mix. At night, air-conditioning blasted from the window vent and I couldn't fall asleep. In the day, when I was too tired to even read the magazines that other passengers had left behind, the driver hit a button and all the television screens came alive with *Sister Act*.

I pressed my forehead against the icy glass and stared at culverts and blown truck tires and state police cars parked side by side in the valleys of highway medians. Was anyone really looking for me?

A large man fell asleep on my shoulder, his whole body sagging toward me. And I didn't move. I stared out the window, and because it was night and my reading light was on, I could see only us. And if you were sitting across the aisle, you might have thought we were a couple.

I always remembered who I loved, though I was traveling farther away from them each minute. I thumbed through mental pictures of Jack and Barb like a POW trying to keep his mind straight. Jack's head pressed on her hip. Her hand resting on his shoulder, that look of worry on her face. I wondered if she had changed her mind about me. I wondered if she hated me now.

In Jacksonville, I made a phone call. Barb answered. She knew it was me. She said so. But I wasn't ready for her to tell me never to call there again. I've called her many times since, but I still haven't spoken a word.

# CHAPTER 20

IT'S DECEMBER AND I'm standing in the Western Union office in Ormando Beach, picking up a thousand dollars that Eric wired me. I've been staying up in Sebastian, at Captain Jim's Motor Inn.

No more bus for me. I'm traveling in style. By the time they track me down, I'll be dead anyway. Besides, it's not like I'm on the FBI's most wanted list for shooting Tony in the foot.

I stuff the envelope in the back pocket of my pants, my leather sandals slapping at my heels. I climb back into the red Chrysler Sebring and wonder if it was such a bright idea to rent a convertible in Florida.

"Holy shit," I say, arching off the sizzling seat. I feel like I'm sitting on a cooktop. The steering wheel is hotter than a branding iron. I lower myself back down and wince. Test the gear-shift knob with my finger before putting it in Drive.

One quick look in the rearview mirror as I pull out on U.S. 1. I look like I've been on a hunger strike, but the tan and white stubble on my cheeks makes it work. With the shades on my sweaty face and the orchids rippling on my silk short-sleeved shirt, I could pass for a charter boat captain with a substance abuse problem. In Florida, you can be anyone.

It's all part of my last half-baked plan. It's a long shot, but it's better than dying on a Peter Pan bus.

Pulling into the parking lot of Captain Jim's Motor Inn, I take the same blazing parking space I pulled out of an hour before and walk through the lobby, which is pretty much just a hallway with some cream-colored furniture and a basket of complimentary oranges on the concierge desk.

"How are you today, Mr. Hawser?" the pudgy brunette says.

I like using an alias. Paul Mauro might be on his last legs, but I'm Dirk Hawser. The name came to me through thin air. Solid. Indestructible.

"Hanging in there, sweetheart," I say, because Dirk would say something like that. I lick my finger and peel off three fifties, settling up for tonight.

"You're all set," she says, handing me a receipt.

"Question," I say. "My wife and kid are coming down in a few days. Where do we go? Epcot or the Kennedy Space Center?"

"Honestly," she says, smiling sheepishly, "I like Gatorland."

"I think my kid would, too," I say.

I want her to ask about my kid. Dirk Hawser wants to tell her all about Jack. I've been keeping it all inside for almost a year. I'm beginning to crack.

"Here's a brochure," the girl says, handing it to me.

I thank her and head straight to the kidney-shaped pool, where Dirk Hawser has been scorching himself, day after day.

Not a cloud in the sky. Nothing to prevent the sun from beating down on me. I lie back on the lounge chair and read the Gatorland brochure, which makes the place sound a whole lot more interesting than Epcot. For starters, there are the sheep carcasses, fed to the alligators at noon.

Jack would love it. Barb would pretend to be horrified, peering at the bloodfest through her fingers. We'd leave with I'VE BEEN FED TO THE GATORS T-shirts and a stuffed reptile and Eric'll wire me another thousand and I'll blow that on Jack, too. Whatever he wants to do.

I lay the brochure on the ground, thinking of all the other things we'll do here on the Space Coast. Petting farms and Indian River cruises and go-karts.

"He lies out there every day," a woman's voice says. One of the two ladies with the identical striped shirts and long shorts, huddled under an umbrella on the other side of the pool.

They're right. I do. The sun roasting my eyelids and feet. Drying out my mouth. Anything's better than sitting in that nice, cool room, staring at that phone, trying to work up my nerve to call Barb again.

I toss the Gatorland brochure to the hot concrete, watch a warm breeze drag it into the pool.

Captain Jim's Motor Inn has its own infomercial that runs over and over again on the television in my bedroom. A chesty, weathered blonde with an Australian accent is standing in the banquet hall.

"Have a wedding reception in the Tiffany Room," she says. A bride and groom gaze into each other's eyes.

"Dine on seared ahi at our award-winning restaurant," she says, wrapping her fingers around a brass handle and pulling open a door. Inside, it's the newlyweds again, eyes widening as an enormous seafood platter is brought to them.

"Or get down at the Sand Bar."

Is that a lifeboat? I wonder. The newlyweds are getting smashed.

I watch the infomercial over and over again, unable to move.

Barb must have a new boyfriend, I tell myself. Why wouldn't she?

The sun is setting over the palm trees in the parking lot. The traffic on U.S. 1 could almost be mistaken for the sound of the ocean, which is two miles away. I can hear the dress shoes of older couples on the walkway outside. Probably dressed in blazers and patterned dresses, slowly making their way to the seared ahi.

I pick up the phone, place it back down in its cradle.

I can see him. Jack's got a new father figure. Not some dying fugitive who gets excited about the Gatorland brochure, but a solid character with a strong chin and a quick smile who can teach a kid to throw a curveball.

For a terrifying moment, I doubt everything. My love for them. Their love for me. There's nothing but the chipper voice of that Australian woman on TV, dragging me from room to room, showing me the same actors, again and again.

I get up, push open the balcony door, and stare down at the brochure floating in the pool. The two ladies are playing cards now. I could just jump. How bad would it hurt, a three-story fall?

A lot, I think. Besides, it would be a really shitty way to interrupt their card game. I clutch the cold metal of the sliding door and pull it closed again. Pick up the phone. Stab the nine. Then I quickly dial the other numbers before I can change my mind again.

I lie down on the bed, the cord stretched across my chest.

"Hello," Barb says.

For a minute, I don't say anything, but she doesn't hang up.

"Paul," she says. "Is that you?"

"Yes," I say. "I'm in Florida."

This time it's Barb's turn to be silent.

"I miss you," I say.

I can't hear a sound on the other end. Was that a click? Did she hang up?

"Hello?" I say. "Hello?"

"We miss you, too," she says. "You want to speak to Jack?"

"Sure," I say, wiping my eyes. It's like my face suddenly has a bladder control problem. I'm soaked, but she doesn't know.

"Where are you?" Jack says. He sounds extremely angry.

"Florida," I say, barely managing to get the word out.

"Can we visit you?"

"Of course," I say. "That's the whole point. That's why I'm here."

I've always found happiness to be the strangest thing. It seems so simple the moment it truly happens. As if it had been there the whole time, just waiting to be called on. Happily, I pace the room, babbling directions, telling Barb I'll pay for everything. And then it occurs to me, I haven't asked the most important question of all.

"How's he doing?"

"It's been rough," she says.

Me and airport bars. You can't keep us apart for too long.

I'm having a very expensive double shot of Maker's Mark at one of Orlando International's many bars. Being December, it's packed with refugees from the Northeast. An odd mix of chatty senior citizens and exhausted parents. A couple near me is having such a fierce argument that they've stopped keeping tabs on their little girl, who's pushed her own tiny pink baby carriage, complete with limp doll, out to the concourse.

"Great," the woman says, sneering at her husband. "Here comes the psycho look."

"People are listening," he hisses back, jerking his chin toward me.

"Excuse me," I say politely, putting down my drink. "Is that your daughter, by the big plant?"

I watch her husband race across the carpet and drag his daughter and her baby carriage back. The second he touches her fingers, she starts to bawl.

I turn back to the bartender, who rolls her eyes at me.

"It never ends," she says.

Or begins, I think, looking at my watch. Jack and Barb's flight is already forty minutes late.

"Thanks," I say, when she hands me the check. "But I think I'm going to have another. Logan Airport is having a snow delay."

"Just pray it isn't canceled," she says, pouring me another shot of bourbon from the shot spout above her. Not a drop more or less.

"You get the Weather Channel?" I say, nodding at the television in the corner, tuned to the Georgetown game. Who's watching it anyway?

The bartender changes the channel and I add another five to her tip. I lean back and watch the radar wind itself over New England, the last blots of green wiping themselves away.

Jet Blue Flight 574 arrives two and a half hours late. I park myself right against the yellow strip that cordons us off from the gate area. The waiting was a cinch after I knew the storm would clear up, but this is ridiculous. It seems to take a day before the first passengers trickle into the terminal. Then another day before the next group straggles out. Every strange face only makes me more anxious for the ones I'll recognize. All around me, people are leaning over one another's shoulders, patting and hugging. A white-haired man takes his daughter's bag, the same way I'll take Barb's. A boy clamps his arms around his mother's leg and smiles shyly at his grand-father, who's kneeling on the carpet. Then it stops. No more passengers emerge through the door. I'm waiting next to a limo driver holding an index card in the air.

THOMAS HALE, the name scrawled on it says.

"Probably some idiot standing in the aisle, block-ing everyone," I say.

The limo driver nods warily at me and takes a step away. Four more people come walking out. A soldier, narrowing his eyes, as if someone should have been waiting for him. Then two flight attendants, waving good-bye to each other with their fingers. And finally, Thomas Hale, who nods at the driver and follows him down the concourse.

I stand there for twenty minutes. I stand there until the guard sitting near the metal detector slips off his seat and asks me who I'm waiting for.

"My wife and son," I say. "They're on Flight 574."

"Flight 574 is disembarked," he says.

"That's impossible," I say, "because they're on that plane."

He holds the walkie-talkie to his mouth. A gate attendant is closing the door. The red letters that said Boston have been erased.

"Yeah," the security guy says, giving me a funny look. "Got a man standing here who says his wife and son are still on the plane."

"Everyone's off," a voice barks.

"Sorry," the security guy says.

"Fuck them," I say to myself. I'm sitting in the con-
verted lifeboat of Captain Jim's Sand Bar, drinking a
gin and tonic.

One nice thing about Captain Jim's. No one seems to
mind if you curse to yourself. You can dig the heels of your
dress shoes into the sand, and the cover band is always
free. And what makes the fact that Jack and Barb have
blown me off even more palatable is the celebrity sitting to
my left. I've never been very good at recognizing celebri-
ties, but this one, there's no doubt about who she is.

"You're the Captain Jim girl," I say to the weathered blonde sipping the raspberry daiquiri. She's sitting on the other side of the lifeboat, all alone.

She raises her chin, acknowledging me. Then we
turn back to our drinks, nodding our heads to the beat.
I wait until the song ends.

"You did a great job," I say. The last time I saw her,
I was crying like a baby. I decide to keep this information to myself.

"It's a living," she says, in that familiar Australian
accent. Implants, I think. Fortyish. Probably screwing
Captain Jim himself. I've seen him around.

"What other films have you done?" I say, sliding
over to the free stool between us.

"One for the Sea Breeze, up in Kissimmee," she says. "The Singing Gull in Melbourne. The Best Western in Crystal River."

I arch my eyebrows, trying to look impressed, and wonder where the waitress is. Is it possible to spend my last five hundred dollars on alcohol? In one night? Couldn't we load up on booze and push this lifeboat into the Indian River, me and her, and toast the vanishing coast?

Within a few minutes, we're leaning on each other, whispering into each other's ears. I mention Hollywood, which instantly dampens our conversation, but she's not going anywhere, and pretty soon she gets over it and we're whispering again. The band launches into another power ballad by the spotlit palm trees.

Suddenly, it's like the wind's been knocked out of me. I'm at the airport again, watching the gate attendant pull the tan door shut. No Barb or Jack.

"I'll be right back," I say. "I have to make a phone call."

I walk across the sandy floor, buffeted by an awful guitar solo, every bent string having a nervous breakdown. It isn't until I make it to the pay phone by the hostesses' lectern that I realize one shoe is gone, scuttled somewhere in that cool sand. I empty all the change from my pockets into the coin slot.

The phone rings four times. Ten. Eighteen. I stop

counting. Hang up, I tell myself. You're running out of time. Find your fucking shoe. Bring another gin and tonic back to the lifeboat.

I do. And then, half an hour later, with a handful of borrowed change in my hand, I call again.

"Hello," Barb says.

"What happened?" I yell at her.

The silence routine. I'm not falling for this again.

"Let me speak to Jack," I say to her.

"Paul," she says softly. I can feel it in my stomach before she says it. The terrible news is already leaking from my first name.

I hang up before she can tell me that Jack is dead. I have this crazy idea suddenly. It's just a problem on my end. I just have to hang up and everything will be all right.

So I slam the phone down and look down the alley of tiki torches, throwing off more oil than flame, which lead to the lifeboat and the cover band and the green light in the green palm trees on either side of the stage. And I can feel these trivial details burning themselves into my brain, so that I'll always be able to punish myself for being so far away.

# CHAPTER 21

I'VE NEVER BEEN to a funeral. Isn't it odd? Not my father's or mother's. Not even the occasional dead friend. I escaped them all. And, in a sense, standing in the parking lot of Our Lady of the Fields Church in Coventry, watching the whole town file in, I'm escaping this one, too.

It's one of those modern churches, or might have been when it was built in the sixties. Tan bricks. No windows. A slanted roof. One long splinter of a stained-glass window.

I lean against the hood of someone's car in the freezing cold and watch the bottleneck at the church door. Everyone wants to be here. It's a child's funeral. They come along only every few years. And those who are filled with universal grief anyway, for themselves, for Peruvian orphans, for soldiers who get killed overseas, for wild dogs that moan at night, they'll be bowing into the first pew by now. Those are the people I fear most. The ones who'll cry for anyone.

There's the brunette from the hospital and the short bald guy. All the time-wasters who crowded into Jack's hospital room, their frozen breath mixing together. Tony's there, too, limping slightly, I'm glad to see. His girlfriend files in after him with her fat son in his confirmation blazer. A few more people follow, and then I see Barb.

She's pregnant. It's mine, I'm thinking. It has to be.

It makes me so happy that I have a two-minute coughing fit. I look like I can't stand how funny something is. I'm actually stamping my feet. By the time I've calmed my throat down, my palm is slick with green saliva.

But Barb's too far away to even notice me wringing out my hand. She lets an older man take her arm. She's dressed in black, but her face is paler than ever. So pale that her red lipstick seems to float in the air. The man looks at her to see if she's ready and she ducks her chin and walks in.

The doors are closed.

I'm left to imagine the funeral. I'm left out here with the parking attendant and the driver of the hearse, who's having a loud argument on his cell phone, red from his Adam's apple on down. Life goes on.

But who'll recognize me anyway? I ask myself as I move closer to the door. A late-arriving mourner.

One hundred and twenty-five pounds now. I have to stand still whenever I cough, and even the gristle of facial hair on my chin looks grim. I'm wearing a stolen brown jacket with a gash in the collar and a pair of grayish canvas sneakers. Jack would have loved the outfit. I look like a homeless college professor.

I push open the doors, the wide doors, which make no sound at all, which seem to push themselves. And the first thing that hangs me out to dry is the coffin.

Small. Shiny white. Brass handles.

Someone is speaking already. The syllables echoing off the slanted walls. The voice pausing carefully, being witty and sad and articulate, but I don't hear a word.

I'm trying to picture Jack. His eyes, his hands clasped, a pair of brand-new shoes. His Minnesota Vikings cap.

I want to speak to Jack. I want to tell him I was wrong. This isn't all there is. It has to fit into place somewhere. I don't know how, but it does. Maybe I'll find out when I've finally stopped making mistakes and being the worst role model a kid could ever have.

Barb looks over her shoulder, as if she could hear these thoughts. The incessant babble that's always going on in my head.

And she smiles at me. Sadly, quickly, but all the same, a smile. Heretically beautiful. Then she stares straight ahead and I can see her breathing. Her shoulders moving up and down, as if the world were suddenly packed with too much oxygen.

I lower my head and clasp my hands. I nervously dig around my pockets and, finding an old, stiff piece of Dentyne, a tangle of bank receipts, remember these pockets aren't even mine. In a way, I'm already gone. I'm already dead.

The congregation rises and I open a hymnal, lost in a thicket of voices. Some ostentatiously straining to be heard, others doing their best to stay disguised. And they call this joy.

My voice is weaker than the rest. A joke, really. A whisper. In a few months, I'll be as quiet as Jack. My thin hands clasped. Frowning at myself as they turn up the flames.

I weather the rest of the funeral. Try not to think of him. Lock my gaze on that thin strip of stained glass, imagine the craftsman who soldered it into place. He wasn't wasting time. Now that's a profession I might have picked. Coloring light.

Before it's over, I stand up and leave. There's still enough self-preservation left in me. The selfish prick who would like to avoid, if possible, being arrested. I walk so slowly out the door, as if I were stepping over crushed glass. Unfolding my sunglasses, I lay them on the bridge of my nose and start walking back toward the blindingly white Saturn I stole from a senior citizen outside New London. I calmly waited for him to finish the worst job of parallel parking I'd ever seen, and then I just demanded his keys. As far as I'm concerned, if it takes you an hour to park between two cars, you deserve to have your vehicle ripped off. Anyway, he didn't put up much of a fight. I guess he realized I was just saving him from himself.

I see them in the last row of the parking lot.

Two detectives in a black Buick Cutlass, idling near the Dumpster. Someone must have called, or maybe they were there the whole time. It's not the biggest surprise in the world to tell you the truth. In fact, I expected it. But you never know how you're going to react until it happens. Kind of like cancer.

I walk slowly to my car, pausing for another ridiculous coughing fit. Why don't they arrest me now, while I'm playing "Taps" on my fist? Why even let me take the keys out of my pocket?

I unlock the door, climb in. I'm safely back in the vaguely intestinal, plush red interior of the Saturn.

Tapping my rearview mirror an inch to the right, I can see them still sitting there. Fat gray shadows, a fat hand tapping a cigarette out the window.

Maybe they're calling for backup. State troopers. SWAT team.

Or maybe they have no idea I'm me.

I start the car and pull away, easing over a speed

bump as the first of the mourners begin to file out. I start to take the FUNERAL card off the dashboard and then, thinking the better of it, I push it back in the window. I do twenty miles an hour in a school zone, and then I floor it.

And, of course, they're flooring it, too. The flaring headlights of the Buick ping-ponging back and forth, a red flashing light twisting on the dashboard.

I pull a hard right on Route 3, listening to the tires' first shriek of protest. I'm doing a hundred by the time I reach the Bald Hill Road intersection, where I once turned right with Jack to go to the Warwick Mall, his feet kicked up on the dashboard. I'm sailing through the sparse traffic as if everyone were at a standstill.

All right, I'm lying. It's a Saturn. The detectives are practically pushing me along by the time I make the pond. I swerve toward the shoulder, and suddenly I'm aimed in the direction of a woman wearing a white leotard with glinting sequins, skating backward on Johnson's Pond, her long arms enticingly pulling the air along.

Unless that's an angel, the last person who's going to see me alive is a fucking ice dancer.

Me, in a car with FUNERAL in the windshield, wearing sunglasses and three days' worth of grizzle. And even as I swerve off the shoulder and go airborne, I'm thinking, I hope this works, because I don't want to have to do it again.

But when the car impacts on the ice and the airbag comes farting out and the windshield shatters and the hood buckles up so I can't see anything at all, I realize I'm still alive, doing doughnuts on Johnson's Pond, staring at the ice dancer every time I make a circle, the birds already scattering in one long white rippling wave.

And I can see it in the ice dancer's face. Even from here.

What have I done?

But here I am, dear reader. And here you are, spinning along with me, all the way out to the thin ice. All the way out to the middle of Johnson's Pond. Where I do, finally, come to a stop.

I think a second must actually pass. Enough time to feel the wind through the broken windshield. Enough time to lick my cracked front teeth. Enough time to look out the side window and realize the spooked birds are already lazily floating back down into the bare trees, as if they were imitating leaves. They could have waited.

Staked out in my ridiculous coffin, in my stolen jacket, bleeding profusely behind my wrecked sunglasses, I wonder if the ice dancer in the leotard, now skating away as fast as she can, will tell some newspaper reporter exactly where I went under so Barb and the kid I'll never meet can skate over me years from now.

Because the ice is breaking. Freezing water is filling my shoes. Shooting up my calves. I'll never know if it's a boy or a girl. Whether he'll break bottles on this frozen lake when he gets older, or smoke pot on a humid summer night and imagine he sees bubbles.

Now's a fine time to figure out the future of the world. Now's a real fine time to finally show an interest.

And isn't this a fine way to go, me and Jack buried on the same day? But he's the one who finally dragged me down with him. I wouldn't have it any other way. Sinking, I look up, still wearing my wrecked sunglasses, still holding the steering wheel, my mind still feeding me useless details, as a mind will.

Cloudless sky. Wonder if someone lives in that hut? Look at those two people standing by their bicycles, pointing at me.

I'm squinting through my sunglasses as the car begins to sink to the bottom of Johnson's Pond. The sun laid across that hole in the ice like a giant, shiny nickel. It has no intentions of following me into this blackness.

Why are you smiling?

I'm glad you enjoyed it. You in the passenger seat, looking at me so calmly, blowing pinprick bubbles. Even now I have to say, I admire your audacity. Sticking around until the final minute, just to make sure I'm through. Well, I am. This is it. We've reached the silty bottom, the back tires touching down, and then the front. The sunlight the size of an actual nickel now, the ice already freezing over.

P.S.

Insights,
Interviews
& More . . .

# A Conversation with Matt Marinovich

Marian Marinovich

*Where do you live, Matt? I suppose you're going to say Brooklyn?*

I do live in Brooklyn.

*All right, so you live in Brooklyn. How original. Where would you like us to believe you were born and raised?*

Actually, I was born and raised in Manhattan, on the gritty streets of the Upper East Side.

*Was your childhood distinguished by any extremes—by any shameful precocity or appetizing delinquency?*

I was kind of a teacher's pet in eighth grade. I made up for it by getting kicked out of boarding school the following year. I thought I'd fit in better if I drank, smoked pot, and got low grades. I still got picked on.

*What do your parents do?*

My mother is enjoying her golden years. She's probably sitting on her terrace somewhere in West Palm Beach right now, watching alligators cross the golf course. My father passed away, but he was a doctor.

*I've unearthed a 1997* Salon *article in which you make a clean breast of having worked "as a copyeditor for a family-oriented Web site." The article was pleasingly subtitled "Vaginal pears and iron maidens are child's play compared to the dreaded job of a family Web site copyeditor." Care to elaborate?*

I likened it to medieval torture. And that was before I came back to live in New York and started copyediting at women's magazines. I can't say anything bad about them, since I've been treated well at these places, but it's pretty hard to focus on an article about a woman's contraception options at one in the morning. I found myself staring at a photograph of the female condom, trying to understand.

*You worked in a slaughterhouse for a couple years, too, no?*

No, but maybe I should. I need the material. ▶

❝ I was kind of a teacher's pet in eighth grade. I made up for it by getting kicked out of boarding school the following year. ❞

## A Conversation with Matt Marinovich
*(continued)*

*All right, my mistake. Tell us about some of your early jobs, though. And take care to make them interesting—we're accustomed to P.S. authors with remarkable job histories (Joni Rodgers was a "bull semen dispatcher"; Louise Erdrich, a "flag-waver for a road crew"; Russell Banks, a mannequin-dresser at a Montgomery Ward department store).*

At one point, right after college, I was getting fired everywhere. I got fired as an assistant at *Interview* magazine because I didn't dust the managing editor's phone correctly. Nobody should ever be forced to dust a phone. She also sent me on a mission to find plastic hangers. She was very upset with how long it took me to find plastic hangers.

Which brings to mind another job at a PR firm. I only held it for a week, until I took down a phone message the wrong way. My boss said he wouldn't fire me if I admitted that I was dyslexic. I refused to admit it. I'm not dyslexic. I swear.

*You were a college professor. Did teaching theoretic and nuclear particle physics at MIT stimulate or retard your pursuit of fiction?*

Unfortunately, I was just an adjunct. I taught essay-writing mostly, until I realized that my take-home after one semester was a little more than a thousand dollars. Which is roughly what a sandwich costs in Midtown now.

> 66 I got fired as an assistant at *Interview* magazine because I didn't dust the managing editor's phone correctly. 99

*What has been your fondest experience on a train?*

I think it was when I was kind of nodding off on the F a few months ago and some teenager slapped me on the back of my head on his way off the train. It's the sympathetic looks you get from the other passengers that warm the heart. Sympathetic or maybe just relieved it didn't happen to them. But never sit close to the door. Bad things happen there.

*Are you married?*

I am, to a wonderful Irish woman named Marian. We have two daughters, Anna, four, and Gracie, two.

*How did you meet your wife?*

On a blind date. We played pool at a bar in Boston called the Rattlesnake.

*What kind of a student were you? No, ignore that question. What was the most ill-conceived thing you ever did in college?*

With some other drunk friends, I stole a Do Not Enter sign in Bronxville, New York. The cops caught up to us pretty fast. Since I was the only one holding the sign, I was the one who got arrested. The cop kept calling me "Sunshine." As in, "You think you can do whatever you want, Sunshine?" ▶

66 The cop kept calling me 'Sunshine.' As in, 'You think you can do whatever you want, Sunshine?' 99

## A Conversation with Matt Marinovich
*(continued)*

*In your short story "My Chinese Mother" (5_Trope, March 2005), you describe "buying" a mother: "It was Friday night and I was drunk, wandering up from some bar in the West Village where a glass of wine costs you twelve dollars. She was standing on Canal Street, selling tiny American flags." Does this story reflect a true drinking anecdote?*

No, I've gotten drunk and done some stupid things, but luckily, buying a mother wasn't one of them.

*Incidentally, I particularly enjoyed this paragraph in the story:*

> *I lay awake in a tiny bedroom in the back of the [Chinese woman's] house. At first, I thought I was doing it just because it sounded good. I planned on telling this story to someone in the future. Someone I might love. Someone who would understand that I needed to find myself in these situations. Why? I don't know for sure. In biblical times, a child was pushed down a river in a tiny basket, surrounded by stiff reeds. Can you see him bobbing in that milky blue water, the hum of insects building on either side of him? I was pushed too, but no one will ever admit it, and I couldn't even tell you who it was.*

Thank you.

*You crop up on the* Ploughshares *masthead as a "poetry reader" in 1992. How long did you fill that role, and what is your present relationship to poetry?*

My poetry-reader job was very short-lived. I still write poetry though. I always thought that would be my main focus, so it's strange that I winded up writing novels. I never thought I'd have the attention span for it.

*Have you read any notable works of new poetry lately?*

Robert Lowell always feels new to me. I love these lines in "For the Union Dead": "The Aquarium is gone. Everywhere / giant finned cars nose forward like fish; / a savage servility / slides by on grease."
In general, I feel that there's a lot of savage servility sliding by on grease these days.

*What is your favorite word in the English language?*

Cleft.

*Can fiction save the world?*

I'm not sure it can save the world. But when I read a great book, I'd rather be in that world.

*What is your association with* The Little Book of Bathroom Philosophy? ▶

### A Conversation with Matt Marinovich
*(continued)*

I actually copyedited it, but I think they gave me a writing credit because the text was so confusing. You don't want to be confused when you're reading on the toilet. You want to succinctly understand Descartes and then move on with your day.

*Describe the objects on your desk right now.*

A powerstrip. A lot of wires. DSL equipment. It's not a very welcoming desk. I write at the dining room table.

*Does music play any part in your writing process?*

It played a part in *Strange Skies.* I was listening to "Moonlight Mile" by the Rolling Stones when the plot for the novel clicked. [Read about this on page 10 in "Strange Inspiration, from Cancer to Mick Jagger."]

*What do you listen to?*

Recently, I've been overplaying that Metric song "Too Little Too Late." I also love the Thermals, the Clash, Wire, and of course the Rolling Stones.

*What do you really listen to, Matt?*

Okay, I can't get enough of "I Wan'na Be Like You," from *The Jungle Book.*

66 You don't want to be confused when you're reading on the toilet. You want to succinctly understand Descartes and then move on with your day. 99

My daughter walks away, and I'm still dancing to it.

*What book do you wish you had written?*

*Crime and Punishment* would have been nice.

*Name some of your favorite writers.*

Richard Yates, Leo Tolstoy, James Salter, Edith Wharton, Raymond Carver.

*What are you working on now?*

I just finished a book about a guy who unknowingly marries his own mother (don't you hate when that happens?). It's a contemporary version of *Oedipus the King.* ◞

# Strange Inspiration, from Cancer to Mick Jagger

I DON'T THINK I would have written *Strange Skies* if I hadn't gotten cancer. In 2004, a doctor removed a lump on my arm that turned out to be an adnexal carcinoma. The funny thing is that the doctor wasn't even going to remove the lump, since he was in a rush. So I'm lying on the examining table, telling the doctor that I'd really appreciate it if he could spare the time. He starts cutting into my tricep, and he's getting more and more pissed because it's taking a long time and there's all this squishing and splattering and sighing. While he's doing this, I make the mistake of telling him I'm a teacher, so after he stitches up my arm, he hands me his son's college application essay, as a favor to him. I start making little comments in the margins ("redundant!"), but I've lost a lot of blood and I'm getting dizzy, so the doctor comes in and hands me some smelling salts. Looking back on it, I think he just didn't want me to pass out before I finished making comments on his son's kiss-ass college essay. I really hope I didn't help get that kid into Yale.

Anyway, a little fast-forwarding. The lump gets sent to the pathology lab and it turns out to be malignant. I find out there's a fifty-percent chance of lymph node spread. Once you've got lymph node spread, the situation becomes a little more challenging. After more

> 66 He starts cutting into my tricep, and he's getting more and more pissed because it's taking a long time and there's all this squishing and splattering and sighing. 99

surgery, I spent a terrifying weekend waiting for the tests to come back. I don't believe in God, but I'm not an atheist. I always felt like some benevolent, vague force out there was keeping an eye out for me. You know, making sure that I wasn't scraped off the face of the earth at the age of thirty-eight, with a daughter and my wife pregnant. I definitely didn't think my life would have that type of surprise ending.

Which is where writing comes in. After the shock wore off, and I knew that the cancer was in check, I wanted to get even. I felt like I'd been kidnapped by this arbitrary bad luck, and then just as arbitrarily left on some street corner to get on with my life again. The problem was that I was confused, and relieved, and furious, all rolled into one. Writing for me is where everything balances out. If my world feels like it's tilted at seventy degrees one day, all the ugly details slide down into the writing bin. It catches everything. It's where I eventually sort everything out.

The upside of getting cancer is that you instantly have great material. It's like a free round-trip ticket, just for enduring something that sucked. The problem is that I didn't know how to approach the material. I thought it was fascinating all by itself, and that I could just hand it in.

At first I took a very sentimental, almost autobiographical approach. I remember sitting at my laptop and writing the first paragraph of My Cancer Novel. Let's just say it opened with the main character staring at his ▶

> **❝** If my world feels like it's tilted at seventy degrees one day, all the ugly details slide down into the writing bin. It catches everything. It's where I eventually sort everything out. **❞**

own reflection in a Starbucks window, and that tears were brimming in my eyes as I wrote it. Needless to say, it was awful. I was feeling sorry for myself.

I knew I'd have to take a different approach. When I'd taken that long walk down Third Avenue to the doctor's office to find out the results of the sentinel node test, I'd never been so scared. I had to force myself to keep on walking, and I could barely deal with the anxiety of what the doctor would say when he walked into the room. At the same time, at that dark moment, a voice in my head said, Wouldn't it be funny if you skipped your appointment, just told your wife that you're okay? I think that's when the idea for the character of Paul first came to mind. Someone who would lie at an extremely important moment in his life.

I walked out of the doctor's that day with good news. Paul, on the other hand, pretends it's bad news. He somberly tells his wife he has cancer and then begins having what he thinks will be the time of his life. Several nights later, I was listening to the Rolling Stones song "Moonlight Mile" and it all clicked in my head. As I listened to the song, I had this image of Paul on an airplane, realizing that he misses Jack and Barb, and that he can't get away from caring about them. He had this contemplative look on his face, and I could see him looking out the airplane window, realizing that he was in an unfamiliar place emotionally. Mick Jagger, meanwhile, was singing "I've been sleeping under strange, strange skies."

I've played a lot of other Rolling Stones songs, hoping another novel would click into place that way, but it only worked for *Strange Skies*.

So that's how the novel began to fall into place. It cracked me up, the idea of this ordinary, by-the-numbers guy doing something so craven and outrageous. The humor of it freed me from all that gooey sentimentality. I was so angry and in such turmoil after getting cancer, but I'd finally found the right way to express it. You can see the darkness and anger in the early pages of *Strange Skies*, but the humor in it is critical. It saved me from writing a terrible novel about a guy who's just a victim. It released me from feeling like a victim. It's the story of a guy who decides he's going to take charge of his life, and do just what he wants. I think that came from my own sense of powerlessness after the diagnosis. Of course, the main character, Paul, winds up realizing he can't control anything, especially who he loves. ∽

" I've played a lot of other Rolling Stones songs, hoping another novel would click into place that way, but it only worked for *Strange Skies*. "

# Author's Picks
## Short Stories

I'M A BIG ADMIRER of shorter forms, especially the short story. Unlike my favorite novels, which I can't remember reading more than once, I've read all of these stories over and over. I've studied them like a kid watching big league batting practice, hoping to pick up a little technique. Going through these stories again, I notice that one of them, "Visitors," by Donald Barthelme, is covered with pencil marks. I was trying to learn how he wrote so effortlessly in third person. Each of these stories, though, is a clinic, a master class in writing.

1. **Isaac Babel, "My First Fee."** Babel is one of my favorite writers. Here, a twenty-year-old proofreader who can't get laid hires a prostitute for the first time. The humor of that premise alone would make me buy it. Then we meet Vera. Babel's characters are always stubbornly three-dimensional. There are never any sanded edges. Reading him, I always feel like I'm about to learn the dirtiest little secret.

2. **Leo Tolstoy, "Alyosha the Pot."** Blows *Forrest Gump* out of the water. An unsentimental, deeply affecting story of a handicapped man falling in love. It's in the third person, but feels as if it were written in the first; the simple, declarative

66 [In Isaac Babel's "My First Fee,"] a twenty-year-old proofreader who can't get laid hires a prostitute for the first time. The humor of that premise alone would make me buy it. 99

14

sentences match the thoughts in
Alyosha's head.

3. **Richard Yates, "Saying Goodbye
to Sally"** (from *Liars in Love*).
Alcoholic writer in doomed
Hollywood relationship. Your
average drinking-in-the-afternoon
plot upended by Yates' vivid,
unsparing portrayals of people
who will always make the wrong
choices.

4. **Tobias Wolff, "Hunters in the Snow"**
(from *In the Garden of the North
American Martyrs*). I won't ruin the
ending, but let's just say that you
shouldn't bust your buddy's balls
before you go deer hunting, even
if his name is Tub.

5. **Ann Beattie, "Janus"** (from *Where
You'll Find Me and Other Stories*).
Woman falls head over heels for . . .
a ceramic bowl. One of my favorite
couples in literature.

6. **Thom Jones, "I Want to Live"** (from
*The Pugilist at Rest*). Mrs. Wilson's
cancer has metastasized. The story
follows her from this diagnosis to her
death, in seventeen pages. By the end,
the third person is invisible. It's just
her amazing voice, which makes the
end even more upsetting.

7. **Donald Barthelme, "Visitors"**
(from *Forty Stories*). Divorced
father and his daughter. Melancholy,
funny, pitch perfect. The last ▶

paragraph is beautiful. It's like a story in itself, and a mystery, since it seems to have nothing to do with the previous pages. That's exactly what life is like. You think you've got the gist, and then something completely different hits you.

8. **James Salter, "Foreign Shores"** (from *Dusk and Other Stories*). I can't believe there's only one great au pair story. Here, a little boy is heartbroken after his nanny is fired. ("Best line" award goes to the mother: "They always love sluts.")

9. **Raymond Carver, "A Small, Good Thing"** (from *Where I'm Calling From*). Twisted baker gets his comeuppance. What to read when you think the whole world is wicked.

10. **Samuel Beckett, "Krapp's Last Tape."** It's a very short play that feels like a story. Old man with tape recorder, going over the laundry list of his life, until he gets to a single, lovely memory at the heart of it. It's the way he starts, stops, and repeats it again that always kills me.

> " I can't believe there's only one great au pair story. "

Don't miss the next book by your favorite author. Sign up now for AuthorTracker by visiting www.AuthorTracker.com.

16